The
Debs

Susan McBride

The Debs

DELACORTE PRESS

Published by Delacorte Press
an imprint of Random House Children's Books
a division of Random House, Inc.
New York

Visit us on the Web! www.randomhouse.com/teens
Educators and librarians, for a variety of teaching tools, visit us at
www.randomhouse.com/teachers

Library of Congress Cataloging-in-Publication Data
McBride, Susan.
The debs / Susan McBride.—1st ed.
p. cm.
Summary: Rising high school seniors and life-long best friends Laura, Mac, and
Ginger hope for invitations to be introduced to Houston, Texas, society as Glass
Slipper Debutantes, while each faces family and boyfriend issues and Jo Lynn
plots Laura's downfall.
ISBN 978-0-385-73519-3 (trade pbk.)—ISBN 978-0-385-90508-4 (glb edition)
[1. Debutantes—Fiction. 2. Interpersonal relations—Fiction. 3. Wealth—Fiction.
4. Houston (Tex.)—Fiction.] I. Title.
PZ7.M478276Deb 2008
[Fic]—dc22
2007051590

The text of this book is set in 11-point Berthold Garamond.

Book design by Trish Parcell
Printed in the United States of America
10 9 8 7 6 5 4 3 2 1
First Edition

To all the girls who've ever felt less than perfect,
had their hearts broken, been left out, made mistakes,
or suffered at the hands of a Queen of Mean:
this one's for you.

The Glass Slipper Club
Debutante Program

Overview of Rules

- Ten qualified girls (Rosebuds) will be selected each year, the first week of Pine Forest Preparatory's fall semester, to comprise that season's Glass Slipper Club Debutante class.

- Debutantes must be in good standing academically and must demonstrate high morals.

- Regular meetings will be held the first Monday of each month from September through May. The year will culminate with the Rosebud Ball the last weekend of May.

- The debutante class will receive training in deportment and dance and will attend specially arranged functions, such as teas, luncheons, and philanthropic events.

- All debutantes will be daughters or granddaughters of members of the Glass Slipper Club or will be sponsored by an active GSC member.

- Parents, grandparents, or guardians of debutantes are required to make a $12,000 donation to the Glass Slipper Club Foundation.

- Each family of a selected debutante must purchase a table at the Rosebud Ball.

- Each debutante will select a young man of quality to be her peer escort to the ball. However, her father (or another male family member) will present her.

- Debutantes are responsible for purchasing their own ball gowns* and gloves and for the cost of professional photographs. (*In order to ensure that no two Rosebuds' gowns are alike, prior to the ball each gown will be cataloged for reference.)

- During their debutante year, all Rosebuds must dress appropriately, per GSC Selection Committee standards, with no visible tattoos or piercings (other than a single piercing in each ear) and no excessive use of makeup.

- Debutantes should follow proper etiquette and exhibit ladylike demeanor during all GSC events (for example, no chewing gum, eating with hands, etc.).

- Rosebuds must maintain a "clean" lifestyle and refrain from using drugs and alcohol.

- If a Rosebud demonstrates blatant disregard for GSC standards, an appointed member of the Selection Committee will speak with her. Should said member so recommend, the board will be notified, as will the girl's mother.

- Should the board deem it necessary, a debutante may be removed from the program, and eligible girls on the waiting list will be considered to fill the vacancy.

Houston is, without a doubt, the weirdest,
most entertaining city in Texas,
consisting as it does of subtropical forest,
life in the fast lane,
a layer of oil,
cowboys and spacemen.
—from a Texas tourism guide

Texas debs are a law unto themselves.
—Karal Ann Marling,
Debutante: Rites
and Regalia of American Debdom

The rich are a lot of crumbs
held together by their own dough.
—Lorenz Hart

When life gets tough, eat cookie dough.
—Laura Bell

One

Laura Delacroix Bell grabbed the armrests of her seat in a death grip as the Southwest Airlines jet touched down at Houston's Hobby Airport, the wheels bumping hard against the tarmac before rolling to a stop. The kid behind her let out a wail loud enough to split her eardrums, and she gritted her teeth, willing the Flight from Hell to be over with ASAP.

Ten more minutes and I'll be off this cattle car, she told herself, thinking that nothing would feel better than stretching to her full five feet nine inches after her cramped ride from Austin. Besides getting a major crick in her neck, she'd been stuck smack in front of the crying child, who'd kicked the back of her seat for nearly an hour. As if that wasn't torture enough, all they'd fed her were two tiny bags of peanuts.

"Welcome to Houston, home of NASA, Minute Maid Park, and the late, great Ima Hogg and her baby sister, Ura," a flight attendant in a bright orange shirt and khaki shorts drawled. Laura rolled her eyes, thinking how everyone who'd lived in H-town for more than two minutes knew that Ima Hogg had really existed, while her "baby sister" Ura Hogg was pure hogwash.

The Fasten Seat Belts light blinked off, and Laura instantly freed herself from the nylon straps. She hunched over to retrieve her black patent Dolce & Gabbana tote from where she'd wedged it between her bare feet, then hunted down her pewter Sam Edelman flats before she slipped them on and was ready to roll.

Never again will I fly coach, no matter how desperate I am, she thought, and wished her first-class flight on American hadn't been canceled without warning. She'd had to scramble to catch anything departing at the same time, but it was better than standing around waiting. She had been *aching* to get home, and finally, she was *here,* after two months away from her own bed; her best friends, Mac Mackenzie and Ginger Fore; and anything remotely edible.

If she'd had to spend another week at fat camp, she would've gone totally postal.

They'd made her surrender her precious BlackBerry Pearl upon arrival and had only given her ten minutes of e-mail time on a communal computer before breakfast and after dinner. How the heck could she keep up with TMZ and Perez Hilton *and* stay in touch with her friends in only twenty minutes a day? The counselors didn't even let the inmates watch TV, so she'd missed every rerun of *The Hills*.

Camp Hi-De-Ho was the corny name of Laura's expensive summer prison, though she thought of the place more as Camp Hellhole. There was a reason carrots and lettuce were called "rabbit food." Human beings couldn't survive on the stuff, unless you were a size zero and your name was Mary-Kate or Ashley (either of whom probably considered eating rabbit food splurging).

She turned on her BlackBerry immediately after deplaning,

checking it first for voice mail and finding a message from her mother. *"Hey, darlin',"* Tincy drawled above background noise that sounded like the engine of Harrington Bell's company Gulfstream. *"Hope your trip home is quick and painless. Unfortunately, Daddy and I won't be there to greet you. We'll be at the cabin in Telluride if you need us. Can't wait to see my baby girl again, all fit and spectacular and ready for debdom! Kisses."*

Laura felt a little pang but shrugged it off. Her daddy never liked to stick around H-town in the summer, when it was as hot and humid as a steam shower. So it didn't surprise her that Harry Bell's needs came first, even ahead of welcoming home his younger daughter.

Did that mean Daddy's driver would pick her up?

Laura hated to think of riding in the backseat of a smelly cab, especially after being squashed amid the hoi polloi on Southwest long enough to make her crave a leisurely soak in a vanilla-scented bubble bath.

She sighed as she looked up her text messages next, finding one from Mac that brightened her mood considerably:

Talked to UR mom. Ging & I will pick U up. C U soon!

Well, well, well. Maybe her karma didn't need an overhaul after all.

Laura smiled, sticking the Pearl back into her D&G bag and rummaging for her compact. She checked her teeth for any trace of peanuts and did a quick repair of the liner that had smeared around her wide-set blue eyes. She ran her fingers through her straight blond hair before she tucked the strands behind her ears. A touch of Stila daiquiri glaze on her lips, a tug on her gray tee to make sure it covered the white of her belly that her low-riding True Religion jeans didn't; then she took off, striding away from the gate, suddenly dying for fresh air, no matter how muggy it was—and August in Houston was *always* muggy.

Can't wait to see my baby girl again, all fit and spectacular and ready for debdom!

Her mother's words stuck in her head as she walked. More than disappointment, she felt relief that Tincy wouldn't be around for a few days, likely until after school had already started. As for her father . . . well, Laura didn't see him much as it was. He ran his plumbing parts business with a tight fist on the reins and was forever jetting somewhere on business. When he wasn't, he spent long hours at his downtown office, often not getting home until Laura was fast asleep. But Tincy Bell was another story entirely. She was the classic Helicopter Mother, hovering about and keeping tabs on everything from Laura's friends to her GPA to her weight. And lately, Laura's weight had been the touchiest subject of all.

What would Ma Bell do when she realized Laura hadn't lost a single pound in two months? Would she cut off Laura's platinum AmEx? Deny her their traditional every-other-Sunday post-brunch mother-daughter mani-pedis at Sensia, with its cool seagrass floors and shoji screens? Get rid of all the Pillsbury Slice 'n Bake cookie dough in the fridge, to which Laura had been addicted to since childhood?

Like the immortal Scarlett O'Hara, Laura figured she'd worry about that tomorrow. Instead, she shrugged off her apprehension, silently repeating her personal mantra, which Mac had claimed she'd partially stolen from the old Popeye cartoons: *I am who I am.*

Someday, she decided, after she died, she was coming back as a lizard, the kind that lived in Mexico and spent all day lying on rocks in the sun. Lizards surely didn't live to please their overzealous mothers.

Of course, Laura knew what was making Tincy so nervous these days—why her hypersensitive mom had insisted on sending her to fat camp—because it was making Laura anxious, too: "D-Day," also known as "Deb Day" among their social set.

This year at all-girls Pine Forest Prep—her *senior* year—would entail more than the usual aggravations of the ugly plaid skirts that made her butt look twice its size, the whispers and dirty looks from übersnob Jo Lynn Bidwell and her Bimbo Cartel, and all the charitable work Tincy made her do to pad her prep school transcript. (Not that Laura *minded* candy-striping at Texas Children's Hospital or doling out food for the Bread of Life, so long as it didn't take up every single minute of every weekend.)

What had Laura most preoccupied was knowing that shortly after school resumed on Monday, invitations would go out to girls selected by the Glass Slipper Club to be this season's crop of debutantes. The GSC was an ultra-exclusive women's organization made up of socialites, mostly the nouveaux riches from Houston's Memorial Villages, or "the Bubble," as some liked to call the upscale area nestled between I-10 and Memorial Drive where Laura and her friends lived. And every image-conscious Glass Slipper Clubber, including Tincy Bell, held first and foremost the commandment that "thou shalt be neither debu-trash nor a debu-tank."

It was the debu-tank part that had Laura gnawing on her French manicure, as she knew it meant anyone over a size eight.

Laura wore a fourteen.

She owed her height and big bones—and the sizeable

trust fund waiting for her when she turned eighteen—to her father. But even her mortal enemies couldn't deny that she was pretty, which put her at two for three, since good looks counted for nearly as much as money, which mattered a smidge more than being skinny.

Still, Tincy Bell was determined that *nothing* would stand in the way of Laura's following in her footsteps and becoming a Rosebud. If she was honest, Laura had to admit that she was as eager to debut as her mother was to make it happen. Being a debutante meant more than just the whole tradition angle, with its touch of Old Moneyed gentility so coveted by New Money (and *everyone* Laura knew in the Bubble was New Money). Being a GSC deb was the shining star Tincy had been guiding Laura toward since she was a little girl, the fairy princess moment of her high school life, the chance to *be somebody*, to wear a gorgeous white couture gown, elbow-length gloves, and a diamond tiara in her hair without having to say "I do" to anyone or take over the throne of a fledgling monarchy. Basically, it was the pinnacle of teen-girl worthiness.

What was there not to like about that?

So a little suffering was nothing. And she'd survived, hadn't she? Camp Hellhole had toned her up with all those morning hikes, for sure, and the Cadbury bars she'd smuggled in, hidden inside boxes of thinkThin bars, had kept her from fleeing the campgrounds to find the nearest Circle K. As Laura saw it, life would be unbearable without chocolate. It'd be almost worse than a world without boys.

"You need a hand with your bag?" asked a tattooed guy in a blue uniform, cutting into her thoughts just as she exited the main terminal at the baggage claim. She waved him off.

The glass doors slapped closed behind her, and the humidity

wrapped around her like a wet blanket. It had been hot in the Hill Country of Austin, even with occasional breezes coming off Lake Travis, but that was kid stuff compared to Houston's damp heat. Houston wasn't called "The Bayou City" for nothing, and it truly felt like living in a swamp sometimes, with the sky-high humidity, drenching rains, and ever-present cockroaches and mosquitoes. Still, all that damp made for a whole lot of green, and Laura loved the lush landscape, so Southern and gracious, with Spanish moss that dangled from giant cypress trees, deep-pink azaleas everywhere, the smell of gardenia filling the air, and pines that seemed to soar high enough to pierce the clouds. She didn't mind the mild winters either, and could only remember one Christmas when it had snowed. Barely a trace of white stuff had stuck to the ground, but it had been enough to bring the city to a standstill.

Though winter seems a long way off, Laura mused, standing outside the airport terminal and looking around for her ride, sweat dripping down her face and sliding down her spine. *Ah, there they are!* Her gaze fell upon a familiar metallic gray Prius idling in the pickup zone, its horn tooting and its occupants waving madly. Laura's mouth broke into the biggest grin she'd felt all summer long as she watched the passenger door pop open and Mac Mackenzie flew out at warp speed.

"Welcome back!" her friend shouted as she nearly knocked Laura over with a bear hug, and they squealed in unison, holding on and rocking from side to side like they were doing a demented tango. "Feels like you were gone forever," Mac blurted out. "I still can't believe you and Ginger both bailed on me for the summer! If y'all ever go take off like that again, I'll have to kill you. Even Alex abandoned me." She pouted.

"You mean the Geek Next Door didn't stick around to play Dungeons and Dragons?" Laura teased, laughing as they drew apart.

Mac swatted her. "Hey, lay off Alex! He doesn't even play D and D anymore."

"Oh, geez, my bad."

"Besides, he just got back from Europe." Mac set her hands on her boyish hips and exhaled loudly. "It was, like, the loneliest summer ever, and you have to promise it won't happen again."

"Okay, how about this?" Laura cleared her throat and held up three fingers. "I swear I'll never go back to fat camp, not even for Tincy. Scout's honor."

"Damned right you won't." Mac straightened her smart-girl glasses, which sat crookedly on the tip of her sunburned nose. Her dark hair was as wild a mess as ever, and she had on ink-smeared shorts and battered Old Navy flip-flops. "Besides, you're fine just the way you are, so stop letting your mom try to make you over into Mini-Tincy. Didn't she already do that to your sister?"

"She tried, until Sami escaped to San Francisco." The bee-otch had packed her bags and moved barely a week after graduating from Rice University, Laura recalled, which was when Tincy had begun fixating on Everything Laura. "I hate to think what my mother's gonna say when she realizes I'm pretty much the same old me."

Mac gave her a stern look. "Cut yourself a break, why don't you. Stop obsessing over what Tincy wants! Anyway, Ginger's having a BFF-only sleepover at the Castle, and I don't want you pouting all night. That's an order."

"Yes, ma'am." Laura felt like saluting but giggled instead.

Some things never changed, she thought. Mac was just as blunt as she'd been in kindergarten, when they'd all had to share margarine tubs filled with finger paints. Mac had given directions then and she was still doing it now.

"So we're taking the clown car, huh?" she asked as Mac nudged her toward the Toyota hybrid, Ginger waving from behind the wheel. "Couldn't the Green Girl get something earth-friendly with a big enough backseat that my knees didn't smack into my chin?"

"Stop, it's not that bad," Mac chastised, then glanced around. "Hey, where's your luggage? I've never seen you travel lighter than at least two full-sized Louis Vuittons."

"I shipped my trunk back with FedEx, and I hope they lose it," Laura confessed as they headed toward the car. "It's all gray T-shirts and sweatpants and sensible panties. Nothing silk with lace or high-end labels." She made a face. "It's a wonder I didn't break out in hives."

"Well, you got a tan, at least," Mac said, trying to console her.

"More like a golfer's tan. It ends at my sleeves," Laura told her, hearing Ginger Fore drawl, "Hey, girl!" as Mac opened the front passenger door.

"Did Mac mention the sleepover at my place tonight?" Ginger bent over the console to ask her.

"Yeah, and you're on!" Laura said, leaning in past Mac and smiling at Ginger's freckled face, almost not recognizing her with a pixie cut—what had happened to the red ponytail she'd had at the start of June? She was ready to comment on it, but Ginger shouted "Hop in and let's bounce!" before she could get the words out.

So Laura popped open the back door, about to toss her

bag inside, when a speeding sports car with a growling engine did a nosedive into the space behind them, tires screeching and horn blasting, so that Laura jumped, hitting the top of her head on the frame of the Prius.

"Ow." She stood upright, wincing and dropping the tote bag at her feet. She muttered, "Freakin' idiot," but nearly stopped breathing when she realized the offending vehicle was a customized burnt orange Corvette Z06 with vanity plates that read:

GR8HANZ.

Oh, God.

It was Avery Dorman.

What was he doing at Hobby Airport on a sweltering Saturday afternoon?

No way was he there to play welcoming committee, unless there were strings attached (and they were usually the kind that pulled her like a puppet).

She swallowed hard, thinking that she knew those GR8HANZ intimately, just as she knew that the burnt orange color of his 'Vette was for the University of Texas. Avery had committed to the UT Longhorns and he'd be playing for them next year after he broke the school record for receptions at the all-boys Caldwell Academy this season, which everyone *knew* he was bound to do. He was the resident Golden Boy, drawing crowds so big to Friday night football games that Caldwell Academy had been forced to shift locations from their school's athletic field to Tully Stadium, which could seat fifteen thousand instead of a mere couple thou. Avery was royalty in a place where football was king. And on top of it all, the guy was a certified Grade-A hottie.

Laura had known Avery since their mothers had enrolled

them in the same ballroom dancing class when they were four-teen. He was about the only boy she hadn't towered over, con-sidering that, even as a freshman, she'd stood nearly six feet tall in heels. They'd learned the fox-trot and flirted like crazy until Avery had finally asked her out a year later. Once he had, Laura had fallen hard, so in love she'd snubbed Mac and Ging entirely so that she could spend time with Avery and his crowd.

Until one awful night when the world had blown up in her face. Laura had been too embarrassed to talk about it, not even to her two best friends, which had left Mac and Ginger believing that Avery was at fault and Laura was better off without him. But it wasn't Avery who'd humiliated her. Only Laura knew exactly who was responsible: Jo Lynn Bidwell, the Queen of Mean.

The past is history, Laura reminded herself, thinking that she had too much ahead of her to dwell on it now. She'd made some big decisions at Camp Hellhole and had written down a list of priorities for her senior year. At the top was becoming a Rosebud, of course. Second was getting Avery back for good. Everything else, including revenge, could wait.

Laura wondered if Avery's showing up at the airport was a sign from above, one she shouldn't ignore.

"Girl, let's go," Mac prodded from inside the car, her head stuck out the window. But Laura found she couldn't move.

The sleek Corvette parked cockeyed behind the Prius demanded her attention, especially when Avery got out, scooted around the hood, and approached her. His sandy brown hair looked sun-streaked against his skin, and his tanned arms, fully exposed by his muscle tee, were rock hard. He was one of the few guys she'd ever been attracted to who made her feel small and dainty and feminine.

"Why, it's Laura Bell," he said as he planted a palm on the trunk of the hybrid and leaned against it. His gaze swept up and down Laura's body, making it feel a whole lot hotter than ninety-three degrees in the shade. "Man, you're looking good these days." His dimpled smile made her heartbeat skip. "How about letting me give you a ride home?"

"Hmm, last time I saw you, I ended up staring at your taillights, and now you're offering me a lift?" She cocked her head, hooking a thumb in her pocket, hoping he couldn't see how badly she was sweating. "How'd you even know I was getting in this afternoon? And don't tell me it's some amazin' coincidence."

Like perhaps his latest plaything, Camie Lindell, was tied up getting detoxed with a high colonic, so he needed a temporary distraction.

"A little bird told me you'd be arriving," he teased, looking and sounding a lot like Matthew McConaughey in his *A Time to Kill* prime.

"What little bird?" Laura knew good and well it wasn't Mac or Ginger. They'd nicknamed Avery "Ratfink" long ago.

"I called your house to see what was up, and your mom's girl, Babette, said you were just getting in at Hobby," he explained in his smooth, smooth drawl.

Laura grinned. Calling Babette her mother's "girl" made it sound like they were lesbians or something, when Avery knew exactly what Babette was to Tincy. The woman kept Tincy's schedule, something that was no small feat, considering how much Laura's mother loved throwing herself onto every chichi fund-raising committee that would allow her on board (and there were plenty—a generous donation from Harrington Bell went a long, long way).

"I shot out here like Jeff Gordon, wanting to catch you before anyone else did."

He jerked his chin toward the Prius, and Laura followed his eyes to see Mac hanging out the front window, frowning like Debbie Downer. "Tell me I'm not too late."

"Well, um, I . . ." She wanted to say that she was leaving with her two BFFs, that she hadn't seen them *forever* and she'd missed them terribly. But the words seemed to stick in her throat.

"*Laura.*" Mac tried again, scowling. "Don't," she said simply. Laura knew what she meant: *Don't go with him, he's bad news, he dumped your ass and broke your heart, and he'll do it again and again and again if you let him.*

"Pretty please," Avery said softly.

Laura gazed into his playful eyes, which seemed to see right into her soul . . . and right through her clothes at the moment. Okay, so maybe he had an ulterior motive, she told herself, but then again, who didn't? She knew she'd be a fool to refuse. He was too damned good-looking to blow off—at least, that was her reasoning.

Laura turned to Mac. "Sorry, chica," she blurted out, and began talking fast so she wouldn't have a chance to think it over twice. "I'll meet up with y'all later at Ginger's house, okay? I can't wait to catch up on every little detail of how your summer's been!"

"*Laura!*" Mac shot her a desperate look, but Laura averted her eyes, grabbed her bag, and closed the door to the Prius.

Avery stood beside the 'Vette, smirking knowingly and holding the passenger door open.

Laura hurried over to him and got into the car as gracefully as she could. The thing was so low to the ground, it took almost gymnastic maneuvering. Avery jumped behind the wheel and had the sports car in gear before Laura had even buckled her seat belt. Was he afraid that she'd change her mind if he didn't leave quickly?

"Babette said your parents flew to Telluride, so you'll be going home to an empty house. I figured I'd hang around while you get settled in." His right hand left the wheel to settle on her thigh, and his fingers gently rubbed the stretched denim. "Then maybe you could slip out of those hot clothes and put on those white debutante gloves your mama gave you, and . . . well, you know how imaginative I can be."

Good. God.

If she'd been an old-school belle from gentrified River Oaks, like Ginger's grandma Rose Dupree, she would've swooned or at least had the decency to blush a vivid pink. Not that the comment left Laura unaffected. Her mouth felt like cotton. How she found her voice after that she'd never know; when she did, it sounded like a croak.

"Your imagination is exactly what concerns me," she said, pausing just long enough to make him sweat—or at least wonder a bit—before she told him, "Sure, we can hang out for a while."

As they drove off, shooting past the gray Prius, Laura hoped like hell he couldn't hear the frantic flutter of her heart above the roar of the engine.

She thinks Bosnia-Herzegovina's
the Wonderbra model.
—Isabel Wolff

Why doesn't *America's Most Wanted*
search for the thief who stole
my stepmom's brain?
Please, get it back.
She needs it desperately.
—Mac Mackenzie

Two

"Unbelievable," Mac said to Ginger, watching as the vanity plate on the back end of Avery Dorman's burnt orange Corvette disappeared into traffic well in front of them on Airport Boulevard, heading toward I-45. "The Ratfink shows up, snaps his fingers, and Laura turns into a dishrag. Aren't modern women supposed to be *beyond* falling for guys who're wrong for them? It just makes our whole sex look stupid."

"That's what it's about exactly, Mac"–Ginger nodded–"sex. You can't rationalize biology."

"It's like nobody can keep their pants on anymore. Whatever happened to romance and candlelight dinners and guys courting girls with love songs and poems? My mom used to talk about how my dad wooed her with flowers and mix tapes before she even let him kiss her."

"Courting and wooing? Poems and mix tapes?" Ginger laughed. "Talk about old-fashioned. You should really stop reading all that Elizabeth Barrett Boring–"

"*Browning,*" Mac corrected her, leaning closer to the vents so she could feel the cool air on her skin. She closed her eyes as unruly hair blew across her face.

"Whatev," her friend replied. "No matter how badly you want it, the Victorian age isn't coming back."

"Hooking up is *so* prehistoric," Mac insisted, ignoring Ginger's dig. She leaned back in her seat, crossed her arms, and stared out the window. She didn't care if she was labeled *old-fashioned*. It was better than being called a ho behind your back and letting your emotions get all messed up by players who didn't want anything more than a fast you-know-what, to say nothing of running the risk of catching some funky disease. "You think Laura'll be okay?" she ventured to ask.

"Sure. Until Avery disappears again and she finds out he's dating some other girl, just like all the times before this."

"If that's what being in love is all about, then I hope I never fall for anyone, not that way," Mac said, adding under her breath, "unless he's the complete opposite of Avery Dorman."

She valued brains over brawn anyhow; exploits in academia over prowess on a football field. What did women see in guys like the Ratfink, except the obvious? Mac much preferred someone like, say, Alex Bishop, who was the exception to the rule that said every guy at Pine Forest Prep's "brother" school, Caldwell Academy, was a stuck-up jerk like Avery. Alex was cute in an "I'm not hooked on steroids" way and he wasn't afraid of being pegged a geek. Mac might have even liked him beyond the "we're just friends" stage if they hadn't grown up side by side. When your baby album contained pictures of you at three taking a bath with the boy next door, it sort of killed all sense of mystery.

"Well, Lord knows I can hardly sit in judgment of Laura's bad taste in guys, can I?" Ginger said, her eyes wide. "Not after some of the choices I've made."

Mac wondered if she meant Enrique the Married Spanish Tutor or Mark the Emo Guitarist, who was, like, twenty-seven and who'd thought that scamming on groupies was a rock band's God-given right.

Just as Mac was about to remind Ginger of the idiocy of both crushes, Pink's "Stupid Girls" blared from the car stereo, and she decided to keep her mouth shut.

> *Stupid girls, stupid girls, stupid girls*
> *Maybe if I act like that, that guy will call me back*

Before Mac could do it, Ginger tapped the audio controls on the steering wheel and switched the radio station to 94.5 The Buzz, catching Velvet Revolver in the middle of "Let It Roll," just as they were singing *"burn her out of my head, drink her off of my mind,"* which Mac found rather ironic as well. But she felt less mad at Laura somehow, after taking Ginger's words to heart.

"In a way, Laura and Avery are kind of perversely roman-tic. She's like Pam Anderson with Tommy Lee," Ginger opined with a toss of her spiky red hair. "She thinks she's done with him, and he just keeps coming back like—"

"Hepatitis?" Mac finished for her.

"I was thinking more like poison ivy." One of Ginger's freckled hands left the wheel to scratch a spot on her neck, causing a dozen recycled-metal bangles at her wrist to jangle. "In fact, I'm wondering if I might've wandered through a batch down in New Orleans. Building houses for Habitat isn't all fun and games, you know."

"Oh, really?" Mac cracked a smile. "What'd you do, roll around in the bushes with that senior from Tulane you kept e-mailing me about, the guy who always took his shirt off when he used the nail gun?"

Talk about boy crazy. Ginger was nearly as bad as Laura, only, so far as Mac knew, she didn't have her eye on any particular guy at the moment. Ging was more into causes these days, like building houses for the homeless or saving the planet.

"Ah, Hayden the Hunky Hammerer. He's *so* the flavor of last month." Ginger snorted loudly, the noise completely incongruent with her tiny Tinker Bell exterior. "I struck out with him anyway." She sighed. "The dude decided I was far too young and immature and blew me off for a premed student at Emory." She shrugged. "Can I help it if I have a thing for older men?"

"He said you were too young? No way."

"I know! D'you believe?"

Nope, Mac had a hard time buying that one. Wasn't it every man's dream to bag a younger woman?

She frowned and resumed gazing out the window at the industrialized edifices, strip malls, and sad-looking houses that lined the interstate. Billboards sprang up one after the next, half of them in Spanish and many of them beer ads that featured blondes with ginormous breasts. Living in the Villages, she sometimes forgot how big Houston was, how beyond her pretty green neighborhood was a port city with a shipping channel and Galveston beach a mere hour away, not to mention all the millions of people from different cultures spread out in every direction and the endless gray miles of highway.

"Isn't your dad a lot older than your stepmom?" Ginger asked, drawing Mac's attention away from scenery that was anything but charming.

"Yeah, like eleven years, I think," she remarked, hating the edge she heard in her own voice. "She's barely older than we are."

"More like your babysitter than your mom, huh?"

"Tell me about it." Mac shifted position, drawing her knees up so she could rest her feet on the dash. Her unpolished toenails looked like they could use a good buffing.

"Is Honey still making you nuts?" Ginger asked, clicking on the blinker as she changed lanes, merging onto I-10 West. "Have y'all called a truce, at least? I mean, you haven't put arsenic in her sweet tea yet, have you? Or blown up her tackle box full of Mary Kay?"

"Don't I wish," Mac said dryly, and leaned back against the headrest. "It was hard at the lake house without you or Laura. It was just me, Dad, and Honey." She started scratching at a scab on her shin until Ginger slapped her arm and made her stop. "I kinda hoped Dad and I would get the chance to talk privately, but Honey barely left us alone. And when she did"—Mac picked at a callus on her palm—"he hardly said two words to me."

"That sucks." Ginger's voice oozed sympathy.

"It's okay," Mac lied, and slid her feet down to the floor again. "I'm getting used to it."

It had been that way since her mom died of lymphoma two years ago. Jeanie Mackenzie hadn't felt well for a while and had finally gone in for a checkup at Mac's urging. Six months later, Mac was bawling over her mother's mahogany casket.

All too quickly, Mac's life had been knocked upside down. She'd lost her closest confidante and biggest supporter. In the days and weeks after the funeral, it had buoyed Mac's spirits to hear people remark how much she looked like Jeanie or how they walked alike and talked alike, though she figured that was part of the reason her dad kept his distance. And since he'd married Honey Potts this past spring, he had even less time for his daughter, or maybe more of an excuse not to be around her.

Mac felt sure that he was as broken up inside as she was, and she wished he'd let it out once in a while. But Daniel Mackenzie was as buttoned-up with his emotions as he was with his Brooks Brothers shirts. Jeanie had been the one who'd worn her heart on her sleeve, and Mac missed that. She missed having her mother there; missed the hugs and the kisses on her forehead, missed getting her hair ruffled and hearing someone call her "Mackie."

"Anyway"—she shoved the glum thoughts aside so she wouldn't start bawling—"Honey either clung to my dad like Lycra or skipped around in her short shorts with her big-ass pageant hair, acting all perky and calling me 'sweet pea,' while I imagined her falling off the slalom ski into the algae and being dragged under."

"Snap!"

"Or her blow-dryer exploding and her hair catching fire."

Ginger laughed. "C'mon, Mac. She's not that bad."

"No, she's worse."

"At least your stepmom wants to get to know you. My dad's trophy wife doesn't even want me around." Ginger wasn't laughing anymore. Her mouth tightened and her pale skin turned pink, her blush nearly covering up her freckles entirely. "You know how many times I've been invited to their house in River Oaks? They live, like, two streets over from my grandmother, but do I ever see them? No."

"I'd say you're lucky." Mac tugged a loose thread on her old Bermuda shorts. "I just wish she'd find some project or charitable foundation or something to do besides trying to be my buddy. She's always bugging me to get facials with her or have our nails done, saying things like, 'Oh, but you'd look so much better with a shorter haircut,' or, 'If you'd let me tweeze your brows, your pretty eyes would just pop!' She's such a pageant parrot, and you know how I hate those girls. They're a bunch of sheep in Prada heels and Stila lip gloss."

"Maybe if you'd give her a chance, you'd realize she's not as horrible as you think," Ginger suggested, shrugging. "She seems okay to me."

Mac stuck her finger partway in her mouth and made gagging sounds.

Ginger kept pressing Honey's case. "She tries too hard, yeah, but I'll bet she has good intentions under all that—"

"Spackle?" Mac cracked. "She must've learned how to apply her makeup at Lowe's."

"Never mind," Ginger said, and began looking intently at the highway signs, murmuring, "We should be close to our exit. . . . Yeah, there it is."

Mac looked up and saw the white letters on green, spelling out "Bunker Hill," and felt something relax inside her. Maybe she really was a Memorial Isolationist, which was what Alex liked to call everyone who lived in the Villages

29

and rarely ventured out of the Bubble, except for an occasional foray to the Galleria in Post Oak, to Minute Maid Park for a ball game, or downtown to a museum or the symphony. As a kid, Mac had learned that the Villages had been founded in the 1950s by corporate execs who wanted country-estate living outside the city proper. For the most part, it was their wives who'd started the Glass Slipper Club. Their daughters had been the first-ever Rosebuds. Mac liked knowing the history of the place, and she loved the vibe of living in the burbs. Besides, driving ten miles across Houston meant getting stuck in traffic that could take half an hour or more to wade through, and everything Mac needed was close to home: her house, her friends, her school. Although she wouldn't have minded if her daddy's new wife lived somewhere far away, basically *anywhere* that wasn't the Mackenzies' renovated Colonial off Knipp Road.

"Look, if you want to whine about Honey, it's okay," Ginger said, as if reading her mind, though Mac realized she'd bitched plenty already, maybe too much. She'd been complaining about Honey since the day her father had introduced them.

"The thing is," Mac tried to explain while a familiar bubble of frustration pressed against her chest, "Honey's not my mother, and she never will be. My mom was unselfish and funny and she didn't pressure me to be anyone but myself." She stopped as tears swam to her eyes. God, she hated when she got weepy. She blinked them away, slouching against the car seat and crossing her arms protectively. "I just wish Daddy's new wife would leave me the hell alone, that's all," she whispered. "It's hard enough without having her to deal with."

And if Mac hadn't had a part of her mom to keep with

her, words she carried around every day, she would've felt an even greater loss, if that were possible. Particularly with Honey redecorating the house, removing traces of Jeanie Mackenzie each time she replaced a seventeenth-century walnut side table with a shiny new piece from Ethan Allen, or put a treasured English pastoral oil into storage in favor of an Andy Warhol soup can.

"I still miss her," Mac whispered, and Ginger's right hand left the wheel to squeeze Mac's arm.

"Oh, girl, I'm so sorry. I know you do. Sometimes I forget how you must feel, 'cuz you always act like you've got it under control. But if you ever want to talk about it, let it out. Remember, no secrets."

"I know, I know. But I can't. Not now. I don't want to go there, okay? And if you start feeling sorry for me, I'm going to throw myself out the car door."

"Hey, I'm on your side," her friend reminded her. "You have every right to feel the way you feel, and I don't think you need to change for anybody, definitely not for Honey. You're always the one telling me and Laura to be ourselves, right? You're pretty as you are, besides, and you know how I feel about superficiality. Natural is always better than artificial. It's just some peeps aren't comfortable being themselves. They always want to be someone else. Maybe Honey is like that."

"What she's like is annoying," Mac grumbled. "And you can see for yourself if we stop by the house first so I can pick up my stuff for the sleepover."

"I'll play bodyguard," Ginger offered, hunching her thin shoulders in an effort to look menacing—*As if,* Mac thought—"and I'll keep Honey far enough away so you won't even catch a whiff of her Aqua Net."

31

"Fat chance," Mac scoffed; Honey sprayed enough of the stuff on her do to destroy what was left of the ozone layer.

They tooled down Bunker Hill Road, passing apartments, gas stations, and strip malls, until they turned onto Taylorcrest and, after that, Knipp, where all the yards seemed wide and green and landscaped, almost tropical, with blooming white jasmine and lavender lantana, even palm trees and cypress trees dangling Spanish moss. As the grounds grew increasingly lush, so did the houses, which basically came in two handy sizes: large and supersized.

The Mackenzie residence fell more into the "large" category. The place Ginger's dad had built off Piney Point—way before he divorced Ginger's mom—now, *that* was supersized. It wasn't called "the Castle" for nothing, and Mac had always loved spending the night there. There were so many rooms to explore, so many places to hide where no grown-ups could find you, and Ginger's room even had a turreted ceiling. It was beyond cool.

But first things first.

As they turned into Mac's cul-de-sac, she closed her eyes and crossed her fingers.

"What're you doing?"

"If I'm lucky, Bridezilla won't be home," Mac explained, daring to peek as the car bumped onto the circular drive in front of the House the Bimbo Had Taken Over. "Crap," she breathed, uncrossing her fingers when she saw Honey's midnight-blue Beemer parked smack in front, beneath the shade of a huge old elm. "My luck sucks big-time today, huh?"

First Laura had blown them off, and now this.

She wondered why her stepmom hadn't gone to the country club with her dad so she could hang out with the other trophy wives, sipping vodka martinis and yakking about Botox, backtalking stepkids, and Brazilian bikini waxes while they waited for their hubbies at the 19th Hole. Maybe they'd tossed her out for wearing too much makeup or for bringing back the Farrah Fawcett flip when it should've stayed dead and buried.

"We all have our crosses to bear," Ginger joked, shutting off the ignition and flipping her keys into her palm. Her green eyes flashed impishly. "C'mon, stiff upper lip and all that, like you're always saying to me and Laura."

Mac pouted. "Yeah, but it's more fun when I'm giving the advice, not taking it."

They got out of the Prius, and Ginger followed her to the door. She paused as she jammed her key in the brass lock, remarking, "In and out in five, you got that?"

"Got it."

As soon as they entered, stepping out of the damp heat and into the chilly marbled foyer, a voice rang out. Mac shivered, and she wasn't sure if it was from the blast of artificial cold or from the sound of Honey's voice.

"Mah-*chelle!* Is that you, sweet pea?"

Mac cringed at the syrupy tone, wondering if that was the voice Honey had used when she'd been named Miss Congeniality in the state pageant a couple of years ago, just before she'd latched onto the widowed and wealthy Daniel Mackenzie. Honey *so* overdid the Southern belle routine, right down to her name, which was too sugar-sweet to be true: Honey Potts.

Oh, wait. It was Honey Potts *Mackenzie*, Mac corrected herself, and swallowed down the bitter taste the name left.

Before Mac could say "plastic," there she was, floating

toward them in a cloud of Aqua Net and honeysuckle perfume. *Ugh*. Her father must've lost his mind, marrying such a ditz.

"Hey there, darlin', and Miss Ginger, nice to see you, too." Honey picked her way across the black Carrera tiles in her spike heels, nearly spilling out of her tiny pink top. She gave them both air kisses and even made a bit of small talk with Ginger, asking about her trip to Louisiana, before Mac interrupted.

"Excuse us, okay? We're just here so I can pack a bag. I'm staying over at Ginger's tonight. Laura'll be there, too."

Honey's pink-painted mouth settled into a disapproving frown. "But, Michelle, didn't we have plans for this afternoon?"

No one called her "Michelle" but her teachers at Pine Forest Prep . . . and her lovely new stepmummy.

"Sorry," Mac said, not meaning it. "But I've already promised Ginger and Laura, and I don't remember making plans with you."

And she couldn't imagine having agreed to go, unless she'd been hypnotized.

"Hell's bells"—Honey set her hands on her size-two hips and made a moue, looking honestly upset—"we're all set for deep tissue massage and facials at the Uptown Salon." She cast a critical eye on Mac's sunburned nose. "And not a minute too soon."

Massage and facials with the stepzombie? Mac glanced at Ginger and had to bite her lip to keep from laughing. Was this a joke?

It was the third weekend of August, which in Texas terms meant the final days of freedom before heading back to Pine

Forest Prep for another scintillating year of lectures, homework, and snubs from the Bimbo Cartel. The last thing she wanted to do was waste a moment of her Saturday afternoon at the day spa with Miss Surgically Enhanced Knockers.

"Maybe another time," Mac said as diplomatically as she could, feeling only the vaguest twinge of guilt at the disappointment in Honey's face.

"But I thought we'd do some shopping afterward, too," Honey pressed.

"Thanks, but no," Mac said firmly. She didn't need new clothes, not when she wore a uniform to PFP five days a week; and she had fresh ones—tailored, pressed, and ready to go—hanging in her closet. Her dad's secretary always made sure of it. Besides, it wasn't like she dressed in anything but jeans and T-shirts when she wasn't in PFP's regulation white shirt and plaid skirt. She was hardly Jo Lynn Bidwell, the school's reigning fashionista (and a *total* Oompa-Loompa—was she ever less than perfectly bronzed, even in the dead of winter?). Mac wasn't into labels or spending Daddy's money like it grew on trees.

But Honey sure was. Shopping was Honey's specialty, and she had a stuffed-to-the-gills walk-in closet the size of Rhode Island to prove it.

"Oh, c'mon, Michelle, pretty please?" Honey clasped her beringed hands and held them up like a beggar. "I'd even spring for you to get a haircut." She cocked her head, studying Mac with narrowed eyes. "Your bangs are pretty shaggy, and your brows could use a little pluckin'."

"Mac, I could leave," Ginger said, "and you could come by later, after you're done with Honey. It's no big deal." She slung her hemp bag over her shoulder and took a step toward the door.

"No!" Mac cut her off and grabbed her wrist, not wanting to be left alone with the step-Barbie. But apparently Honey felt otherwise.

"Oh, Ginger, sweet pea, that's a great idea." The blonde clapped, and her six-carat Harry Winston engagement ring caught the light of the Austrian crystal chandelier, nearly blinding Mac with its glare. "Why don't ya go on home and Michelle can join you later."

"Sure, Mrs. M, no problem," Ginger said, shooting Mac a look and mouthing the words *stiff upper lip* until Mac released her hand. "Come by when you're finished, okay? I've got a few things to do in the meantime anyway."

Mac mouthed back, *I will get you for this.*

Her friend smiled. "Later, gator."

Mac stood by helplessly as the redhead gave a back-handed wave before she slipped out the door, leaving Mac with no graceful way out. She released a slow breath, tempted to dash around Honey and her double-Ds and make a beeline up the curving stairwell for her room. But her stepmother caught hold of her arms, keeping her where she was.

Miss Runner-Up Bayou City stared her down and said, "Let's cut to the chase, shall we, sugar? You listen here, Michelle Mackenzie, you'll need to look polished as shoe leather when you're presented at the Rosebud dinner, and you *will* be on the list. I have inside information. Invitations go out this week, and I want you to look your best. You know how your momma wanted this for you. Your daddy told me so himself."

Mac squirmed, hating to agree with Honey about anything. But this time, she was right. Jeanie Mackenzie had wanted Mac to debut. She'd left letters behind, ones that Mac had read so many times the linen stationery was worn soft. She kept her favorite with her always, folded and stuck in her wallet. It laid out all the things Jeanie had wanted for her daughter—things she wouldn't live to see Mac do—and becoming a Rosebud was one of them.

I can picture you already, Mackie, walking out on your father's arm as you're introduced, holding your chin up and smiling, showing the world the kind of woman you've become, beautiful inside and out. You can do a lot of good, baby, and set a fine example for other young girls at PFP. You have so much to offer. I don't think you even know how much yet. And you can believe I'll be watching you, feeling my heart swell, and wishing I could be there beside you to tell you how proud I am of you. . . .

"Mah-chelle, did you hear a word I said?"

She shook her head, unapologetic. "I was thinking of something else."

Something that made her heart clench.

"I asked if you knew what being a legacy meant."

Hello? Did Honey think Mac had an air bubble in her cranium, too? She'd received a nearly perfect score on the verbal portion of her SATs, for God's sake. She knew words that would doubtless cause a short circuit in Honey's brain if she tried to pronounce them.

"I know what it means, yeah," she said, wishing she could explain to Bridezilla that accepting an invitation to the debutante dinner was trickier than just buying the perfect dress at Needless Markup. Mac was all about being herself and not having to prove her worth to anyone, which was

37

why she wasn't sure she was cut out to be a Rosebud. Wasn't it all about showing off, hobnobbing with the likes of Jo Lynn Bidwell, Camie Lindell, and Trisha Hunt, and throwing good money away on an expensive gown that she'd only wear once? But she wasn't about to explain her tangled emotions to Honey Potts, of all people.

"You're as good as in," her stepmother explained needlessly. "Being introduced into Houston society is a huge honor. You never know what'll come from that. It's how your momma met your daddy, so I hear, and I'll be there to watch you every step of the way to make sure you don't stumble."

"*You'll* be watching me?" Mac repeated.

Honey bit her lip, rising up on her toes, looking fit to burst as she announced, "Daniel got me into the Glass Slipper Club, and that nice Bootsie Bidwell put me smack-dab on the selection committee. How sweet is that?"

Whoa.

From what Mac had heard, there was a waiting list to get into the club. And Honey didn't even have a blue-blood pedigree.

"I thought someone had to die for a new member to get into the GSC," Mac blurted out, unable to stop herself. "So who'd my father kill to get you in?"

"Kill? What on earth?" Honey blinked. "What your daddy did was make a *very* generous donation to the Glass Slipper Club Foundation. Oh." She put a pink-tipped finger to her lips, and a grin broke out on her made-up face. "You're just pullin' my chain, aren't you?"

"That depends," Mac replied, her inner bitch surfacing so quickly she didn't have time to fight it. "Are you one of

38

those dolls who won't quit talking unless someone *stops* pulling your chain?"

Honey giggled like a fourteen-year-old. "Ah, Michelle, you're so funny!" She slipped her arm through the crook of Mac's elbow, guiding her toward the front door.

"You and me, we're gonna have the *best* time this afternoon!"

Mac rolled her eyes and prayed to God she'd get through the next few hours without losing it completely and trying to murder her stepmummy with her spearmint Binaca.

Would she have to wear an orange jumpsuit if she committed Honeycide, or could she do blue? Orange– particularly burnt orange Corvettes–made her sick to her stomach.

To us the world is a museum;
to them it's a store.
—Fran Lebowitz

They're not SUVs.
They're Urban Assault Vehicles.
Seriously, what soccer mom really
needs to drive a Hummer?
—Ginger Fore

Three

Ginger's cell started making lip-smacking noises—her text-message alert—just after she'd left Mac's house and climbed into the Prius, which felt like it was 350 degrees. Forget frying eggs. She could've baked veggie muffins in there. The leather seat stuck to the back of her thighs, and her newly shorn red hair began curling against her damp neck.

Get the AC on fast or I'll melt! her inner voice shouted at her.

So Ginger multitasked, starting the car, cranking up the air, and fumbling with her hemp bag, finally fishing out her Razr and finding a new message waiting. She figured it was Laura, giving her a quick 411 on her "ride home" with Avery. Oh, boy.

But when she saw the message, a tiny *ping* went off in her chest.

Where R U? Will U B back soon? Want 2 talk 2 U.

Ohmigawd.

Javier Garcia was looking for her.

Her heart pounded faster than when she'd tried out for the track team her freshman year and had nearly collapsed at the end of the 400-meter.

What could he possibly want to talk to me about? The mural he was painting for Deena in the formal dining room? An upcoming Go Green rally that he was leading?

Or did he want to ask her out? Even though he'd already told her she was too young for him, seeing as he was a senior at the University of Houston and she was still in high school. It was like Hayden the Hunky Hammerer all over again.

She started texting him back, but her thumbs kept hitting the wrong keys so that she ended up deleting more than she wrote. Instead, she dialed his number, biting her lip as it rang once, then a second time.

"Ah, *chiquita,* so there you are, wherever that is," he teased, and she pictured his dark eyes crinkling at the corners as he smiled, his teeth a slash of white against his olive skin. "You out with your homies?"

"I'm leaving Mac's house," she told him, ignoring the way he liked to call her *chiquita*—"little girl." "How long will you be there?"

"Another twenty minutes, maybe. I'm just about finished."

"Finished for good?" Her heart sank to her belly. "Or for the day?"

"Ah, you sound worried, like you'll miss me, huh?" he said, and laughed. "Naw, I've still got a few finishing touches. But for now, I'm cleaning my brushes before I take off. You on your way home?"

"Yeah"—she put the car in gear and pulled out of the Mackenzies' driveway, the cell at her ear—"I should be back in ten. Is Deena there?"

If her mother was around, there was no way she'd be able to talk to Javier alone.

44

He must've sensed the panic in her voice, and reassured her. "Chillax. *Tu madre no esta en casa.* She's probably selling another mansion to one of her rich friends and counting her greenbacks."

Ginger couldn't help smiling. "Ah, so you *do* know her."

"Hell, I'm on her payroll, for a few days more, anyway," he cracked. "See you soon?"

"Yeah, see ya."

Javier hung up, and so did she.

Ginger braked at the end of Mac's street, waiting for a few cars to pass on Knipp Road. Setting her Razr in one of the cup holders, she glanced up and caught a glimpse of her face in the rearview mirror.

She looked flushed, and not from the heat. Just hearing Javier's voice made her nervous, maybe because she'd been keeping him a secret all week long, not even spilling to Mac or Laura because her attraction to him was still so new.

Yeah, yeah. She knew she was breaking their "no secrets" rule—a rule that she'd instituted—but she was afraid that talking about him might jinx things. She'd only just met him at a Go Green rally before she'd headed down to New Orleans. They'd gone out for coffee and ended up at his apartment. They'd sat on his futon, talking for hours about art and music and how to save the earth, with Lucinda Williams's gravelly voice in the background. He hadn't even kissed her.

Two days later, she'd jetted to Louisiana, not sure if she'd ever see him again. Then she'd returned from the six-week Habitat project, walked through the front door, and *bam,* she'd heard his lightly accented voice saying, "Hey, *princessa.*" And there he'd been, painting a mural of the

Provence countryside on the wall of the formal dining room. He told her that Deena had hired him on the recommendation of an art professor at the University of Houston. She liked to believe it was karma bringing them together, not just some fluke.

Every day since she'd gotten back—after Deena went to work—Ginger had hung around Javier before she met up with Mac for lunch or a movie or a lazy afternoon by the pool. She mostly watched him paint and listened to him talk about his plans to save the woodlands, once he'd graduated from U of H with a major in environmental design and a minor in art.

"There's a better way to build our cities without ruining the ecosystems," he'd told her. "Nature was here first, ¿lo entiendas? We're the ones who keep messing up the planet."

Oh, yes. Ginger understood, and she felt the same way entirely.

Curious as hell about what Javier needed to say to her, she floored the accelerator, tires skidding on gravel before gaining traction and propelling her forward as fast as she could go without sliding into a ditch or catching a cop on her ass.

She took a right on Taylorcrest and tagged along behind a Volvo SUV following the speed limit exactly. Sidewalks and grass-filled ditches lined the road on her either side, everything dry now, though she thought of how fast those ditches filled up when it rained. Low-lying Houston seemed prone to minor floods whenever the sky opened up and let them have it.

C'mon, c'mon. Ginger tapped a finger on the wheel as she drove. It was taking forever to reach Piney Point. She hung another right, passing ranch houses mixed with Mediterranean-style villas and contemporary glass-walled structures before she saw the familiar stone pillars and cast-iron street sign for Fore's Way. Her dad had named the street once his development firm had finished construction on the family's monster mansion at the dead end of a long circular driveway made of a special limestone he'd ordered from a mine near Austin. "The most expensive driveway in Houston," he'd bragged way back when, as if a then-six-year-old Ginger had cared about expensive driveways, though maybe it was appropriate, considering they lived in one of the richest zip codes in the country.

She drove her Prius to a stop smack in front of the Castle's mammoth doors, carved and arched and looking like they belonged to some Gothic fortress. Only, there was no moat, just low green hedges of boxwood and lots of wild ferns the landscape crew had put in while Ginger was gone.

Javier's beat-up old Volvo baked beneath the sun to the left of the four-car garage; Ginger didn't see her mother's gas-guzzling Jaguar anywhere, thank God.

She got out of the car, hesitating for a second to squint through the sunlight, gazing up at the stonework and turrets and the thick line of tall pines that encompassed the grounds, feeling very small somehow.

Or was that merely the effect of having a father like Edward Fore, who had always seemed larger than life? The local press liked to call him the Donald Trump of Houston, but Ginger thought of him more as the Chronically Unavailable Father.

She raced up the flagstone steps, unlocked the door, and pushed her way in, at once doubly certain Deena wasn't around, as no Chanel bag sat on the marble-topped table in the foyer and there was no trace of her mother's overpowering White Linen. The chatter of *Oprah* on TV emanated from the kitchen, the usual background noise while Doreen, their longtime cook, began preparations for dinner.

Ginger caught her breath, composing herself, before she crossed the foyer into the dining room, stopping when she saw the nearly finished mural on the wall: the waves of lavender against a verdant field edged with yellow flowers, a charming villa nestled in the background, green trees behind it. *Beautiful* was the only word to describe it. Ginger wished she could paint half as well as that.

"Javier?" she asked the empty room, looking around for him and relieved to see the long, dark Chippendale table and its dozen matching chairs still pushed aside, the canvas tarp covering the planked floor, and the Persian rug that normally filled the space rolled up and set away. The smell of paint hung in the air, but there was no sign of the artist or his brushes.

Ginger cut through the dining room, heading for the rear hallway, which led past the butler's pantry to a side door, so she could see if his Volvo had disappeared sometime in the last two minutes. She was nearly there when a pair of arms reached out of nowhere and pulled her into the mudroom.

Ginger let out a startled yelp.

"Hey, *chiquita*, it's just me."

She turned around and came face to face with Javier. His dark brown eyes crinkled at the corners as he smiled and slowly released her arm. Behind him, on the stone-slab countertop near the sink, his damp brushes were lined up on paper towels.

"You getting ready to leave?" she asked, smiling at the sight of him. The dimple in his chin and the dabs of acrylic paint on his gray U of H T-shirt were too cute. He even had a bit of yellow in his black hair.

"You would've missed me if you'd come five minutes later," he told her. "I can't hang around this mansion of yours for too much longer. It'll start to look suspicious, and I wouldn't trust Doreen not to rat us out, princess."

The way he said "mansion" and "princess," even joking, made Ginger's stomach clench; it was like he was focusing on another divide between them, one that was much harder to bridge than a five-year age difference.

"You wanted to talk to me?" She wiped her damp palms on her denim miniskirt and tugged down the hem of her FREE TIBET T-shirt.

"Yeah, I do." He set his hands on his lean hips, his full lips now unsmiling. "Did you mean it when you said you wanted to help out the cause?" The line of his unshaven jaw looked tightly set, his dark eyes serious and unblinking. "If you're sincere, then I need you to do something for me. Something important."

Which cause? Ginger wondered, because he'd mentioned about a dozen different Go Green projects he was involved with, from cleaning up oil spills in the port and along Galveston's beaches to picking trash out of area creeks to turning junkyards into parks for city kids. But then, it really didn't matter, did it?

"Sure, I'll help," Ginger said eagerly, praying whatever it was didn't involve sewage, dead fish, or spiders. "Um, doing what?"

"Saving a tree," Javier told her simply.

"A tree?"

"The Sam Houston Oak," he said, as if that would explain everything.

"The one in the little park next to PFP that's, like, two hundred years old?" Ginger squinted thoughtfully, not wanting him to think she was distracted by the adorable habit he had of tugging on his earlobe, or by the way his nostrils flared when he was excited about something. "They're tearing it down? Since when?"

"A friend of mine who works in the city manager's office said they're quietly razing it sometime on Sunday evening. The school finally got clearance to use the land—it was donated anonymously for a VIP parking lot. *Bastardos avaros*... greedy bastards," he spat out, and ran his fingers impatiently through his hair before he grabbed Ginger's hand, holding on tightly. "I want you to be there with me tomorrow night when they come to take the tree down. Will you do it? Will you stand up with me?" he asked. *"¿Por favor?"*

He looked so damned intense that it scared Ginger a little, and she thought about reinforcements.

"Should I ask my friends to come, too?"

"Gracias, pero no," he said. "I just need you. And don't tell anyone, *¿comprende?* I don't want your mother talking you out of it."

"I won't," Ginger said softly. She was eager for the chance to prove to him that she wasn't just a spoiled princess who lived in a castle. Maybe this was how to stop being a *chiquita* in his eyes. She needed to have a cause all her own, one that Javier respected.

Well, once she was a Rosebud, she knew, her favorite philanthropy would get a boost from the Glass Slipper Club, and she'd already mentioned to Javier that she might be able to direct GSC Foundation money toward earth-friendly projects, like Trees for Houston, which planted trees all over the city, and the annual Trash Bash, which cleaned up trash in waterways and parks from the Buffalo Bayou to the Houston Ship Channel.

"Can I trust you?" Javier said, gripping her arms, forcing her to look up at him.

"Yes, you can trust me," she answered, as much for herself as for him, her heartbeat loud in her ears.

"*Bueno.*" Javier grinned. His arms suddenly slipped around her as he pulled her close, his warm breath on her cheek as he whispered, "I'll see you at the tree, tomorrow night at seven. I know it sounds early, but we've got to make sure there's still good light and plenty of time for the cameras to roll." He backed away and rubbed her arms before letting her go. "I'll bring the chains and handcuffs. You bring the water. Don't be late. I'm counting on you."

All too quickly, he turned his back on her, putting away his brushes before he took off, ruffling her hair on his way out.

Ginger leaned against the wall of the mudroom, vaguely dizzy, wondering what had just happened. What had she agreed to do? Then again, what did it matter? She would say yes to anything Javier asked of her.

Chains and handcuffs.

That sounded so kinky.

And don't tell anyone.

How was she going to keep this secret from Laura and Mac? She was itching to get on her cell right now and call them, spilling everything.

Ginger left the mudroom on shaky legs, bypassing the kitchen, where Doreen banged pots and pans, and she dragged herself upstairs to her room, a huge round space beneath one of the turrets.

She tried not to think of the practical questions popping into her head, like what if Javier's plans to stop the demolition of the old tree got them arrested? What if Pine Forest Prep suspended her? Scarier still, what if her mother found out?

She made a beeline for the bed and was preparing to throw herself across it when she spotted a box sitting atop the duvet. The return label read "Seasalt Cornwall," one of her favorite online shops, and she plucked the lid off frantically, pulling out a blue-and-green-striped V-neck sundress. A monogrammed note card fell from the tissue, and she opened it to see her mother's loopy handwriting.

> *Here's a little something special for you to wear tomorrow night for supper at your grandmother's house. (Six o'clock sharp, don't forget.) You'll look so pretty, my socially conscious future debutante! I'm out late this evening, so enjoy the sleepover with your friends. See you in the morning (but not before noon!).*
>
> *Love, Mom*
>
> *P.S. It's 100% organic cotton. I didn't see anything I liked in hemp.*

Ginger dropped down on the bed, holding the dress out before her, her smile at her mother's surprise slowly fading when her brain clicked into gear. All of a sudden, she found it hard to breathe.

They were having dinner at her very proper Southern grandmother's house in uptight, Old-Moneyed River Oaks tomorrow at six?

She *had* forgotten. Completely.

Supper with Grandmother entailed a minimum of five courses and lasted for *hours*. How was she going to slip out early so she could meet Javier at the Sam Houston Oak by seven o'clock?

She couldn't do it alone, that was for sure.

I have my bitchy side,
but I don't think I'm really nasty.
I think that a lot of people
probably think that I am.
——Debbie Harry

If pageants have taught me anything,
it's to strike first to stay on top.
Does that make me a winner or a bitch?
——Jo Lynn Bidwell

Four

"Do I have enough oil on my back?" Jo Lynn Bidwell asked the girls sprawled on the chaise longues on either side of her, doing the vaguest peek over one shoulder.

She couldn't very well check things out herself. Her head didn't swivel that far, for one thing, and she'd untied her bikini top, so getting up would mean exposing herself to half the country club. The pool area was packed to the gills even though it was fast closing in on dinnertime.

Jo, Camie, and Trisha had staked out their usual spot near the snack bar at the Villages Country Club hours ago. They'd lubed up their deeply tanned skin with baby oil—a trick Jo Lynn had picked up from her mother, Bootsie—and they'd simmered in the Texas sun for hours, splitting the afternoon evenly between lying on their stomachs and their backs, with occasional breaks to wade into the shallow end of the pool, never diving underwater, God forbid. Who besides the Amazons on the swim team wanted funky green chlorine-bleached hair? As Jo Lynn's stylist, an effeminate man named Zuzu, kept telling her, "Those nasty chemicals will ruin your highlights *and* lowlights, and they'll make you as frizzy as a French poodle! Listen to Zuzu. No pool water for you!"

So Jo Lynn only dipped up to her armpits.

No harm, no foul.

It was almost too bad that school started on Monday, because the rules of summer were so simple: eat, sleep, play with boys, keep your hair out of the chlorine, and tan your butt off.

Jo Lynn was browner than she'd ever been, and the way the lifeguard kept staring at her—Lord help any poor drowning soul—she wasn't the only one who thought she looked ready for the cover of *Maxim*.

"*So?* Do I need more oil? Am I good?" she asked again, impatient for an answer. "We still have at least a half hour of sun before I'll pack it in. Gotta get ready for tonight, you know. My little bash won't put on itself."

She heard a sigh in response.

A dark head raised itself as Camie Lindell got up on her elbows, her full breasts straining against the triangle top of her brown Maya bikini. Her fingers slick with baby oil, she slid her enormous Roberto Cavalli sunglasses down her tiny nose, and her wide-set green eyes peered over the rims to survey Jo Lynn's hindside.

"Looks okay to me. You're shiny from your ass dimples up to your shoulders," she drawled before lowering her bikini-topped torso to a reclining position and tipping her face to the sun.

"Ditto what Cam said. Seems like good coverage from here, too," Trisha Hunt chimed in from Jo Lynn's right. Her strawberry-blond hair was pulled tight off her round face in a floppy ponytail so everyone could see the entwined Gs on her Gucci shades.

"You're shakin' and bakin', Jo-L."

"Okay then." Jo Lynn tried to relax again, closing her eyes. "I trust y'all," she said, which was a total lie.

Jo Lynn Bidwell didn't trust any female, not even her two best friends, something that stemmed from her pageant days, starting back in first grade. Bootsie Bidwell had drilled into her head that other girls were her mortal enemies, her fiercest competition, and Jo Lynn had grown up believing it.

And really, who wouldn't be jealous of her?

She had everything any seventeen-year-old could possibly want, starting with a daddy who sent her and Bootsie to Paris every spring and to New York in the fall for no-holds-barred shopping and who let Jo Lynn use the Bidwell Electronics jet now and then to fly her BFFs to their cottage in the Caymans for long weekends. *Anything for my girls,* he liked to say, though he did as much for Rick, Jo Lynn's older brother. In fact, both Bootsie and Ken Bidwell were in Austin with Rick now, setting him up in his own townhouse so he wouldn't have to rough it in the freshmen dorms at UT.

"So when are the parentals due back?" Camie asked, flipping from her stomach to her back. "Not early tomorrow, I hope."

"God no," Jo Lynn replied, propping herself up on her elbows. "But I'm sure they'll be home by supper on Sunday. Mother has some Glass Slipper Club stuff to take care of before the invitations go out."

Trisha giggled. "I can't believe it's almost D-Day. I want my invite *now,* I swear. I hate the way they make us wait."

"Like, how do you know you're even on the list?" Camie teased. "It's supposed to be a secret, remember?"

Jo Lynn rolled her eyes behind her Prada shades.

Secret, my ass, she thought. Everyone knew which ten girls were getting in and which weren't, no matter how they all pretended it was a great big shock. And Jo Lynn had no doubt her name was at the top of the list. Bootsie Bidwell was chair of this year's selection committee, which meant there was zero chance Jo Lynn would lose her spot.

"So what're you wearing to the announcement dinner, Jo-L?" Camie prodded. "That funky Galliano halter dress your mom bought you in New York?"

"Hmm, I'm not sure yet."

She creased her brow, mulling over several of the insanely expensive outfits procured on her and Bootsie's most recent spending spree in Manhattan. She'd narrowed things down to the beaded Galliano that looked like something designed for a 1920s flapper and the vintage white Valentino with red embroidery.

"Maybe the Valentino," she said, though she knew she wouldn't make up her mind until the last minute.

"Well, whatever you pick, you'll look perfect," Trisha chimed in. "It'll be the icing on the cake for you, won't it? I mean, the guys at Caldwell named you Hottest Girl at PFP three years in a row." Trisha twirled her long red-gold ponytail and sighed. "No other Glass Slipper deb will hold a candle to you, especially not that lard-ass Laura Bell."

Camie sniffed. "She's lucky as hell that she's a legacy."

"And filthy rich," Trisha added.

"Because she's hardly what *I'd* consider deb material," Camie continued without missing a beat. "The girl can't seem to keep her hands out of the cookie jar, can she? It's like she's Pine Forest's version of Ugly Betty. Only she's Big-Ass Betty."

"Yeah, I heard Miss Laura was sent off to fat camp this summer. Your mom's friends with Tincy Bell, right?" Trisha nudged Jo Lynn's leg with a toe. "Did you get an update? Did she lose any weight at all?"

"First, stop poking me." Jo Lynn pushed Trisha's foot away. "And, second, no I haven't heard anything new about Laura Bell. But you know how I feel about sharing the stage with a debu-tank. That'd be, like, sacrilegious. My great-grandmother helped found the GSC, and she'd totally roll over in her grave."

"Can't we do anything to make sure that skank's not picked?" Camie asked. Trisha chimed in with a heartfelt "Yeah, what can we do, Jo-L?"

Jo Lynn reached around her back to retie her bikini top so she could sit up. It was almost time to leave anyway; she had a few things to pick up for her party before she headed home. "Maybe we won't need to do anything at all. Even though Bootsie's tight with Tincy Bell, Laura could still get blackballed by the other committee members."

"Now, *that's* a happy thought!" Cam remarked. Trisha giggled.

Jo Lynn wondered how Laura Bell would take it if she *waited and waited* for a Rosebud invitation . . . and none came. Would she eat herself into oblivion? Would she blame Jo Lynn for everything, like she did last year when Avery Dorman gave her the heave-ho?

As if any of what had gone on back then was Jo Lynn's fault. Laura had brought it on herself, by deluding herself that she'd ever be part of the in-crowd. Though the girl came from money and was well liked at school in the way overly friendly overweight girls were, she was nothing more than debu-trash in plus-sized couture. Laura Bell just rubbed Jo Lynn the wrong way, and *someone* had to show her what was what. If it had to be Jo Lynn, *c'est la vie.*

"Hey, gorgeous." A familiar throaty voice broke into her thoughts. "You look intense. Hope you're not too preoccupied to give your boyfriend a kiss."

"Dillon! What're you doing here?" Jo Lynn nearly jumped up out of the chaise. "I didn't see you out here earlier."

"I just emerged from the cave," he said; Jo Lynn knew he meant the club's weight room.

From the looks of things, he'd finished his workout and decided to cool off in the pool. He was dripping on the deck tiles, making a puddle at his feet. Then he shook his head like a dog and sent droplets flying in every direction.

Jo Lynn took a few to the face and blinked. "You jerk!" she squealed, and sprang out of the lounge chair, grabbing for him.

"Hey, hey, don't make me call the lifeguard," he said, and flung his beach towel around her, rolling her up like a tortilla wrap. "Uh-oh, looks like you're all tied up."

Jo Lynn laughed, feeling light-headed with Dillon's arms around her. "You're such a geek," she told him, which was as far from the truth as she could get.

Dillon was the best-looking guy at Caldwell Academy, by far, with his wavy gold hair and sea blue eyes. Not only was he tall enough that she could wear her spikiest Jimmy Choos and still not reach any higher than his nose, but he was the first-string varsity Q-back, a blue-chip player that universities all over Texas had been actively—if not illegally—recruiting since his sophomore year.

He'd been working out this summer, too, and his biceps

looked carved from stone. His pecs and abs were equally chiseled, and every tanned inch of him glistened as the sun dried the water off his skin.

"Hey there, Cam, Trisha. How're y'all doing? Warm enough for ya?" he asked, and unwrapped his towel from around Jo Lynn.

Jo Lynn watched him turn his boyish smile on her friends, and they were instantly smiling back, murmuring, "Hey, Dillon, yeah, it's real hot out" before they fell silent and stared bug-eyed at him, ogling his hot body.

She bit her lip to keep from laughing. It was almost pathetic, really, the way Dillon could disarm women, no matter their age. Bootsie practically thought he walked on water, which was fine with Jo Lynn. She'd have hell to pay if her parents hated her boyfriend. Luckily, Dillon was everything they wanted for her, and then some—so different from the rest of the Caldwell jocks, who liked to talk tough and drink hard and went hunting on the weekends, shooting Bambi and driving tricked-out Silverados with loaded gun racks in the back window.

God, but that was so cowboy, Jo Lynn thought as she pulled an oversized DKNY T-shirt from her bag and slid it over her head.

Dillon was beautiful and generous and gentle, never trying to outmacho anyone, as was the Texas way. He treated her with kid gloves, acting like the perfect escort whenever they went to the country club for dinner with her folks or dressed up for some charity function at the St. Regis. He would hold her hand, kiss her softly, and put his arm around her in such a way that everyone would coo, *What a beautiful couple!*

"Hey, Jo, you okay, babe? You sort of drifted off there for a moment."

"I was just thinking about us," she told him. No lie.

"Happy thoughts, I hope," he said, smiling down at her, and she smiled back.

"Always happy."

He bent to kiss her, his soft lips brushing hers, and Jo Lynn's heart beat so erratically at his touch, she felt like she might stroke out or something.

Could you ever love someone so much it killed you? she wondered, hoping she'd never have to learn the answer.

"I'll see you tonight, yeah?" he asked.

Jo Lynn reached up to wipe a drip of sweat from his cheek; then she leaned in close enough to whisper, "I figure you'll see *all of me* tonight."

Dillon gave her a squinty-eyed look. "I thought you were having a party."

"Oh, we'll party, all right," Jo Lynn assured him, smiling slyly. "It wouldn't be the end of summer if we didn't, would it? You're bringing Mike and Brody, right?"

He ran a hand through his still-damp hair. "We'll be there."

"Nine o'clock, okay? I'll make sure Nanny Nan's fast asleep by then."

Dillon squeezed her shoulder. "Sounds good to me. You girls don't cook too long out here, okay? I gotta run," he said finally, rubbing Jo Lynn's arm and patting her ass. "But I'll catch you later."

"Can't wait." She nodded, and he ruffled her blond hair before he gave her another quick kiss.

Then he was gone.

"You're so lucky," Camie said, pulling her dark curly hair off her neck and wrapping it into a knot. "Dillon's *très* tasty."

"I'll bet he's great between the sheets, too," Trisha teased, and she and Camie giggled while Jo Lynn ignored them, hiding her true emotions behind her Prada shades.

The truth was, Dillon had hardly been great between the sheets lately; hell, they hadn't done anything but *sleep* between the sheets these past two weeks when they'd been together. Dill seemed alternately exhausted, distant, or pre-occupied. Only, whenever she asked what was wrong, he kept telling her everything was okay.

Just worried about the season and signing with the right college, he'd say, *and getting through the summer two-a-days.*

Jo understood how much pressure he was under. Dillon's dad was a former pro linebacker from the Houston Oiler days. Now Ray Masters was a balding car dealer with a beer gut who'd shifted all his dreams onto his son. Jo Lynn knew that kind of stress firsthand and realized how hard it was on Dillon. That had to be all it was, because he'd never lied to her before, and Jo had no reason to doubt him. But things between them felt weird just the same, and she'd do anything to change that.

She pulled her Marc Jacobs butterfly wedges from her bag and slid them on her slim feet, mulling over what she'd wear that night as she fastened the tiny ankle straps. For sure, something sexy that showed off her assets, something that would ensure Dillon looked at her and *no one* else. Until they could be alone–oh, and she'd make sure they were–at which point she planned to take every piece of sexy clothing *off* and blow his mind.

Then whatever was bugging him would disappear, and everything between them would be right as rain again.

Cockroaches and socialites
are the only things that can stay up all night
and eat anything.

—Herb Caen

Why can't eating Ben & Jerry's
be more like sex with Avery:
sinfully delicious *and*
a calorie burner to boot?

—Laura Bell

Five

"Let me get that for you."

Laura sighed and ceased struggling with the zipper on the back of her mod-print sundress. She glanced at her bedroom's peony-blush walls, wondering if her cheeks nearly matched the deep pink. When her gaze settled on Avery Dorman, sitting on the edge of her queen bed with its ruffled floral spread, she had to blink twice to reassure herself he was really there and not a mirage.

"Stop starin' at me and come on over," Avery demanded in his masculine drawl, the graveled sound of his voice making Laura feel a lot like melting butter.

Demurely, she did as he asked, settling on his thighs and turning her back to him. She pulled her blond hair over her right shoulder; the ends were still a little damp from the shower. She heard a faint swooshing sound and felt the tickle of the zipper going up her spine. Then his hands slid down her bare arms, giving her goose bumps.

"I'm so glad I caught you at the airport," he said, nuzzling the back of her neck, his breath warm on her skin. "I've hardly seen you all summer, and I need my Laura fix."

She smiled, keeping her back to him, relieved he couldn't

see the delight that was surely written all over her face. It would've appeared so gauche for her to jump up and down, knowing that he still *needed* a Laura fix, even though they'd been officially broken up for a year.

Even if she willed her brain to forget him, the rest of her wouldn't. *Couldn't*. Not in an eternity, no matter how hopeless Mac kept telling her she was when it came to him.

Laura happened to believe that some people were meant to be together, and she and Avery were two of them, even if he didn't see it quite as clearly as she did . . . *yet*. But he would, even if she had to work like the devil in the weeks ahead to make it happen. Still, she felt like she was one step closer now.

"There," Avery said, getting back to zippering, "all done." He gave a whistle as she got up off his knee and stood to fasten her belt. "You kick ass in that dress." He cocked his head, and a sliver of sandy brown hair fell across his face. "Only I think I like you better out of it."

"Stop it," Laura said, and blushed despite herself. "You're, like, a pathological flirt, I swear."

"Hey, but I'm no liar." He reached out, catching an arm around her waist and drawing her back again. "I might mean things I don't say, but I never say things I don't mean."

What crazy kind of logic was that?

She wrinkled her forehead, staring at him. "Avery, that hardly makes sense."

"It would if you trusted me a little."

"Trust you?"

"Is that so impossible?" He squinted at her, managing to look halfway serious. "I know sometimes what I do doesn't make sense to you, but it's hard always tryin' to do the right thing when everybody's watching you."

"Don't you mean the *acceptable* thing?" she corrected, because that seemed more like the truth—as she saw it, anyway. He was the Big Man on Campus, the one the guys at Caldwell all wanted to emulate and the girls at Pine Forest all wanted to shag. His image meant everything to him. Maybe too much, sometimes.

"If anyone should get that, it's you, Laura," Avery said, and ran a finger over her hip. "Sometimes I feel like all I've got is people pulling on me. I don't need you doin' it, too."

Laura saw the hurt look on his face and sighed. "I do understand," she told him. "I really do."

She knew how important his success was, not just to him but to everyone around him, including his family, Caldwell Academy, even the Texas Longhorns, since they were setting him up to become the biggest thing since Ricky Williams. Laura realized he didn't get much downtime. She remembered a Saturday when she'd gone over to his house in Hunters Creek to help him babysit his younger sisters. He'd been so silly and relaxed, playing Twister and goofing off, revealing a softer side of himself she was sure other people didn't see. Out in the public eye, he did his tough-guy act, like he always had something to prove; only Laura knew what lay beneath the macho routine. And *that* was the Avery she'd fallen in love with.

"Then stop tugging on me, please," he said quietly. "Let's just enjoy where we are, right this minute."

Normally, Laura would've laughed at such a line, but she didn't now. Her breath caught in her throat as Avery pressed his head against her belly, and she wove her fingers through

71

his hair. Her eyes took in the tangled sheets on her bed and the rumpled white elbow-length gloves discarded on the floor—crazy how those turned him on—and her whole body heated up as she thought about being with him, the way he'd held her, how he'd kissed her, the gentle way they'd made love.

And it *was* love. Deep in her heart, Laura believed it.

Thank God her parents weren't home and Babette was off for the rest of the weekend, because Laura had desperately craved this time alone with Avery after feeling so isolated at Camp Hi-De-Ho. She needed to feel good about herself as she was. It was wrong to think she needed to starve herself to fit in.

She silently repeated her mantra, *I am who I am,* adding a slight twist: *and my heart* needs *this.*

"Listen." She pulled back a step and cupped his chin with her hand, making him look up at her. "I don't want to tug at you, Avery, but I've got something important to say, and I'm only gonna say it once."

Because she barely had the nerve to get it out the first time.

"Okay. I'm all ears." The deep-set eyes within his chiseled face looked at her so intently, like she was the only other person in the world, and she found herself wondering how many girls besides her had seen that same expression; girls who wore a size two, like Camie Lindell and Jo Lynn Bidwell.

It wasn't the most pleasant thought in the world, but it gave her the courage to insist, "You can't keep treating me like a yo-yo. Either we get back together one of these days, or the fun has to end. I don't want to be your bed buddy while

72

you're dating your way through the Bimbo Cartel. I'm worth your undivided attention."

Part of her wanted to take it back after she'd said it, so afraid he'd say, *Well, if that's how you feel, then I'll see ya around, sweetheart.* So she held her breath, awaiting his response; her heart skipped a few beats as well.

"So I'm dating my way through the Bimbo Cartel. Is that what you think?" Avery leaned back on the bed, reclining on his elbows. His bare chest rippled from his pecs to his rock-hard abs; hair soft as down trailed a path down to his waist. He hadn't buttoned up his cutoffs, and she could clearly see his black boxers with the skull and crossbones print. "If you don't believe you mean something to me, I'm not sure why the hell you'd leave the airport in my car, much less come back here."

Laura blinked at him, his reply only confusing her all the more. "It's just that your being here is like a secret," she explained. "It's not like being together in public."

"Your best friends saw us at Hobby. How much more public can we get?"

Laura opened her mouth to say, *They don't count,* but bit her tongue because she didn't mean it like that. Mac and Ginger knew how she felt about Avery. They knew about Avery coming back to her whenever he needed his Laura fix. And they knew she was too weak to refuse him.

What she meant instead was *I want every girl at Pine Forest Prep to know we're a couple again.* Particularly the Bimbo Cartel, if only to prove to Jo Lynn Bitchwell that she couldn't manipulate people's lives, no matter how godlike she pretended to be. It was because of Jo Lynn that Avery had broken up with Laura a year ago. Jo might have been

Avery's first girlfriend, but she didn't *own* him—at least, not anymore. She had Dillon Masters dancing to her tune now, and Laura hated that Avery still listened to a word Jo Lynn said, much less let her dictate his love life. What was up with that anyway?

"I want to go out, Avery," she said, point-blank, "on a real date, or something close to it." Laura set her hands on her hips, waiting. "So what've you got to say about that?"

Avery stared at her for a long moment before he rose from the bed, plucked his muscle shirt from the floor and shrugged it on. He picked his keys up from the silver tray atop her mirrored French dresser. He palmed them and headed for the door.

Just when Laura was about to scream, *I knew it, you jerk,* he paused and turned, lifting a hand in the air.

"Oh, I almost forgot. There's a party goin' on at the Bidwell's guesthouse tonight. If you want to drop by, I'll be there around ten."

"Jo Lynn's having a party?" Laura repeated, hoping she'd heard wrong.

"You remember the address, don't ya, babe? And you know that the guesthouse is by the pool, right?"

"Uh-huh." He knew she did.

"Great. I'll see you there, if you're brave enough to be seen with me in public."

He gave a quick wave, a mischievous grin on his lips, before he sauntered from the room and down the stairs. Laura made her way over to the bay window that overlooked the front drive. The sky was beginning to soften to pink, and gauzy clouds filtered the sunlight.

She pushed back the sheers and waited until she saw

Avery get in his car. The Corvette peeled out of the street in a vroom of engine and a screech of tires, and Laura realized her pulse was screeching too.

Jo Lynn was having a party tonight and Avery expected her to crash it?

She gnawed on her lower lip, trying to figure out what to do. That wasn't exactly the dream date she'd imagined, not by a long shot.

Avery was testing her, wasn't he? She'd given him a kind of ultimatum, and he was throwing one back at her. Was there a way to meet him at the party without Jo Lynn seeing her? Because the witch would relish kicking Laura's ass out if she caught her. The last time she'd been at the Bidwells for a party, Jo Lynn had humiliated her, and Laura didn't want to give her the chance to do it again.

Oh, well. She'd figure something out. She always did.

Laura padded into the bathroom to brush her hair. As she primped, she stared at the picture she'd stuck to the mirror months ago. Its edges were beginning to curl. She'd Photoshopped her head onto the body of a luscious model in a white Vera Wang gown. She'd written ROSEBUD!!! and GODDESS!!! all over it so she could fully envision her dream, not just think it.

"It will happen," she promised aloud, nodding at her reflection. She made herself repeat the phrase several more times, until her BlackBerry chimed, and she raced back into the bedroom to fish it out of her D&G tote. On it, she found a text message from Ginger.

Where R U???

The clock on her nightstand glowed 7:35.

Shiz!

How could the afternoon have gone by that fast? Now she had less than three hours until Avery expected her to show up at the Bidwells' guesthouse, and she hadn't even packed for Ginger's sleepover yet.

Quickly, she texted back: B there N 15. Miss U.

A message came back: Miss U 2. Hurry!!! Pizza on its way!!!

Laura ignored the unmade bed and raced around the room, throwing things in her Vuitton weekend bag, rushing downstairs and through the kitchen, and setting the alarm before exiting into the garage. She tossed the satchel into the tiny trunk of her Mercedes Roadster and backed out, leaving an empty spot between her daddy's Bentley and her mother's Lexus SUV.

As she backed into the driveway and closed the garage door, her cell rang, and her heart leapt, thinking it was Avery. No such luck. It was Tincy, checking up on her from Telluride: "Laura, honey! Did you get home safely? Did you see Mac and Ginger? I know they missed you terribly."

Idling at the end of the drive, Laura did a brief back and forth, mostly saying things like "Yes, I'm fine" and "Yeah, I saw Ginger and Mac at the airport," though she left out the part about Avery driving her home and coming in for a spell. What Tincy and Harry Bell didn't know wouldn't hurt them. Besides, they didn't like Avery any more than Laura's two best friends did.

"See you soon, sweetie. Daddy sends his love. Kisses!"

Laura said goodbye; then she was off and running.

A Gwen Stefani CD blasting on the car stereo, she drove her Mercedes into the twilight as the timer-set lamps popped on one by one and the windows of the Bells' empty mansion glowed pale against the faded sky.

The trouble with trouble
is it starts out as fun.
—Naomi Judd

What if I woke up one morning
and wasn't the good girl anymore?
Who'd keep everyone else out of trouble?
—Mac Mackenzie

Six

"She texted that she'd be here in fifteen, and that was fifteen minutes ago," Ginger said, her words starting to slur at the edges. "I wonder who'll get here first, Laura or the guy from Palazzo's?"

"My bet's on the pizza," Mac replied, and plopped down on the plush pink-and-green-polka-dot loveseat with last year's PFP yearbook in her lap.

She was feeling pretty good at the moment, having Laura and Ginger back in town *and* having received a call on her cell from Alex Bishop on her way over to the Castle. Alex was back after a three-week stint at computer camp in Düsseldorf, and he'd mentioned possibly getting together the next day so she could see the new quad-core Opteron system he'd built. She'd told him yes, of course, not that she really cared about the computer. But she couldn't wait to see Alex again.

"Ah, so you've pulled out the *Pine Cone*," Ginger remarked after putting on her favorite Fall Out Boy CD. She had a thing for Pete Wentz, which Mac didn't understand, because guys who wore eyeliner made her cringe. "Ooo, so are we going to be catty?"

"I figure we need to get some practice in before school starts," Mac said, only half-serious.

Ginger dropped down beside her. "Well, I'm in the perfect mood for it, starved and buzzed." With that, she took another swig of the bottle of chilled Veuve Clicquot they'd swiped from Mrs. Fore's wine fridge, which was always kept stocked to celebrate big closings. Ginger swore one bottle wouldn't be missed.

They passed it back and forth, though it was mostly going *forth*, to Ginger, while Mac flipped through the pages of the annual, picking out photos of the girls they most wished had moved to Uzbekistan over the summer.

In between the champagne and wondering what had happened between Avery and Laura—though Mac could make a highly educated guess—they talked smack about their mortal enemies, the Bimbo Cartel of Pine Forest Prep. Well, okay, the girls in the Bimbo Cartel were everyone's mortal enemies.

"Ohmigawd, take a look at this!" Ginger slapped her hand down on a page. "Is it Jessica Simpson? Or is it Jo-L Bidwell? Hmm, hard to say. Maybe they were separated at birth, though it's too bad they had to share one brain, huh?"

Mac loved when Ginger let go of her "can't we all just get along" attitude, which usually happened when she had alcohol in her system, loosening up her tongue.

She liked it too when Ginger wasn't on her high horse about depleted rain forests or conservation, saying things like "You should brush your teeth and bathe at the same time, and only shower for three minutes or else you're using as much water as a whole African village uses in a day!"

Not that Mac could sit in judgment, since she had her own quirks. Still, sometimes Ginger's ever-changing passions made Mac's head hurt. Last year, Ginger's walls had been covered with posters of rock bands, and she'd been all about black eyeliner and blue fingernail polish. She'd kept her red hair long and straight, like Avril Lavigne's.

Now her hair was cropped short—the rest of it donated to Locks of Love—and her walls were full of Ansel Adams black-and-whites and downloaded photos of that Butterfly woman who'd holed up in a tree; and every bedsheet and stick of furniture in Ginger's enormous bedroom was made from recycled materials, organic cotton, or hemp.

Mac couldn't help but wonder what was next: Retroprep? Disco-glam?

"Look here! See that tiny nose?" Ginger said, and stabbed a finger at a photograph of Jo Lynn Bidwell striking a pose as class president during a student council meeting. "You really think she was born with that perfect snout? I'll bet her daddy bought it for her, just like he buys her everything else, including those ginormous girls she likes to show off whenever she gets a chance."

" 'Ginormous girls'?" Mac wrinkled her brow, wondering if the sips of champagne she'd swallowed had turned her brain to mush, because she didn't know what the heck Ginger was talking about. "You mean Camie and Trisha? They're practically anorexic."

"Not *those* girls, silly." Ginger slapped Mac's shoulder and let out an indelicate snort. "*These* girls," she explained, shoving the bottle between her thighs so she could cup her hands in front of her chest, like she was clutching a pair of melons.

Mac watched the overblown pantomime and could hardly stop giggling to ask, "You think Camie's are fake too?"

"Is the Pope Catholic? Is Tom Cruise an alien?" the redhead cracked before taking a long swig of bubbly. "Is Justin Timberlake black?"

Mac eyed her friend closely, wondering if she'd had enough to drink already.

"Yes, yes, and, *no,* Justin Timberlake isn't black."

"He's not? Well, damn, someone should tell him!" Ginger grinned, spilling champagne on Jo Lynn Bidwell's photograph and then smudging the drops with her finger-tips. "Oops, my bad."

Mac reached over and wrestled the bottle from Ginger's hand. "Girl, you need some food in your system, or you'll be passed out and snoring by nine o'clock."

"I'm fine," her friend insisted, grabbing back the bubbly and taking a generous pull.

"Go easy, why don't you, at least until after we've eaten."

Ginger wiped her damp lips. "Did I ever tell you that you're bossy?"

"Only every day."

"Well, you are." Ginger's gaze fell back on the yearbook. "Oh, hey, there's a shot of Alex Bishop playing at PFP in a chess tournament." She cocked her head, closing one eye as she studied the photograph. "He's really kinda cute, Mac."

"I guess." Mac shrugged.

"Where's he been this summer?"

"He was in Germany for computer camp. He just got back a few days ago." Mac tried to act nonchalant as she said, "He wants me to come over tomorrow and hang out."

She left out the part about checking out the tower he'd built, as it would undoubtedly trigger a "geek next door" remark.

Ginger arched a slim red eyebrow. "You ever think about, you know, getting together with him?"

If she did—and maybe she had, once or twice, fleetingly—Mac wouldn't have told Ginger, not even with their "no secrets" rule. Alex had been Mac's best guy friend since they were kids, and speculating about anything beyond that was . . . well, weird enough to make her palms sweat.

"Wow, would you look at that," Mac said, and quickly flipped to another page. "It's Señor Hernandez and the Spanish Club. You totally lusted after him the whole spring semester."

"Well, I'm not lusting after him now." Ginger's eyelids flickered, and she clutched at Mac's arm. "Want to know a secret?" she whispered. "One I'm not supposed to tell?"

Mac saw champagne slop onto Ginger's thigh and figured she should've taken away the bottle a half hour ago. But it was too late now: the Veuve Clicquot was three-quarters gone, and most of it had gone down Ginger's throat. Oh, well, it wasn't like they were driving anywhere.

"What kind of secret?" she asked, thinking it could be anything.

Ginger spilled some pretty heavy things when she got the least bit tipsy. Like tales of her parents' nasty divorce and how they'd fought over everything, down to who got the dog (Ginger's dad) and who got custody of Ginger (her mom). Mac only hoped it was something less weighty than that.

Her friend leaned in and hissed in Mac's ear, "I'm meeting

Javier tomorrow night at the Sam Houston Oak, only I'm having dinner with Deena at my grandmother's house. So you're gonna have to help me escape."

"Who's Javier?"

"He's been painting the mural of Provence in the dining room—"

"And he wants to meet you at a tree?"

"We're going to save it," Ginger asserted, "so the greedy bastards can't get it to make a parking lot."

Okay, so Javier, the mural painter, wanted Ginger to help him save a tree from some greedy bastards?

Whoa, Mac thought. This secret was beginning to sound like a bad episode of *One Tree Hill.* Wait a minute—they were all bad episodes.

Enough was enough.

"Give me that." Mac lunged for the champagne, wresting it out of Ginger's hands and setting it well out of reach, on the other side of the loveseat.

Ginger pouted for all of five seconds before pouncing on a page in the annual.

"Ooo, check it out." She pointed at a picture of Camie Lindell and Trisha Hunt, saying, "Jo Lynn's toadies *du jour.* You think Bootsie the Stage Mother from Hell has enough clout to make those two Rosebuds too? Ya know, good ol' Boots is chair of the selection committee this year."

"Camie and Trisha are in," Mac agreed, "unless they do something in the next few days to piss Jo Lynn off."

"Like sleep with Dillon Masters?" Ginger stared off into space, tapping her chin. "Hmm, not a bad idea. There are times when I wouldn't mind getting a piece of that myself."

"Which might just get you killed"—Mac nudged her with

an elbow—"skewered with a flaming baton leftover from her pageant days. Something else the Jo-bot and Honey Potts have in common, besides being made of plastic."

"A flaming baton, huh? Think you could roast marshmallows on those things? Maybe we should've asked Honey to join our little sleepover tonight and show us how to do it, unless you wore her out shopping and getting facials this afternoon. You two sheep, with your Prada heels and Stila lip gloss . . ."

"Shut up!" Mac grabbed a throw pillow and smacked her friend soundly.

"You asked for this!" Ginger armed herself and took a whack at Mac.

The doorbell rang.

As fast as the pillow fight had started, it ended.

Mac glanced at her friend, and they both mouthed, *Pizza.*

Instantly, they dropped their down-filled weapons and sprinted from the bedroom, bare feet running up the carpeted hallway and down the wide front staircase, in a race to see who could get to the door first.

Even half-drunk, Ginger won, while Mac dropped onto the polished teak floor, panting like an out-of-breath dog. *Man, I should at least try to get in shape sometime,* she thought.

On her tiptoes, Ginger peered through the peephole and let out an excited "Ohmigawd!" Which didn't give Mac a clue as to who was out there: the pizza man or Laura.

Ginger unlocked the door and flung it open wide, revealing a tousle-haired Laura in a chic Lilly Pulitzer sundress, smiling and clutching a Louis Vuitton weekend bag in one hand. In the other, she balanced a large cardboard box from Palazzo's that reeked deliciously of cheese and garlic.

"Yeah, yeah, I know I'm seriously late, but I intercepted the pizza dude, so the grub's on me," the tall blonde declared, her cheeks flushed a most telling shade of "I just did it with Avery Dorman" pink. "So what do you say we get this party started? Anyone up for a game of Truth or Deb?"

Laugh and the world laughs with you.
Cry and you cry with your girlfriends.
—Laurie Kuslansky

If I ever need an honest opinion,
I ask my BFFs.
My mom always tells me
what's "best" for me.
But my friends will give it to me straight.
—Ginger Fore

Seven

"Come on, pull harder. It *has* to fit."

"For God's sake, I'm doing the best I can," Laura shot back, fumbling with the tiny pearl buttons on the back of the white full-skirted dress Ginger had shimmied into moments before. "Your grandmother must've been a twig to wear this, and even then she must've had to put on one of those things you lace up and squeeze until your waist is, like, twelve inches around—"

"A corset," Mac tossed out from halfway across the room where she sat cross-legged on Ginger's bed. The trio's resident bookworm had a copy of *Jane Eyre* in hand.

Like she hasn't read it twice already, Ginger mused. It was on Mrs. Godfrey's Literature for Senior Girls list, sent in the mail with the "Welcome back to Pine Forest Prep" letters delivered the week before.

"Maybe you could have a couple ribs removed," Laura suggested. "Then I might get the last fifty buttons done."

Frustrated, Ginger sighed and stared at her reflection in the full-length mirror. "Maybe I just need Spanx."

"Ging, you're a size *nothing*. You don't need Spanx,"

Laura muttered, and tugged so hard at the material that Ginger was afraid it might rip. "What you do need is a shoehorn. Was your grandma a midget or something?"

"Now I wish I'd picked Truth," Ginger grumbled.

"You and me both. This is hot work." Laura blew at several limp strands of hair that had fallen into her face. "Next time, don't chicken out on telling us what color panties you'll wear under your dress, and you're good. Truth is always so much easier."

"Oh, really." Ginger gave her a look, wondering if Laura realized what she'd said. *Naw*.

Since they'd devoured the pizza—and Ginger had sobered up—they'd been playing Truth or Deb, a game Laura had invented last spring when buzz about the coming Rosebud selection started heating up. On Ginger's last turn, she'd gone for Deb, which meant a dare that involved something debutante related. Usually, they made each other attempt the Texas Dip, the nose-to-the-floor curtsy they'd have to perform after they were announced at the ball. This time, Laura had ordered her to "put on something white that was worn by a Rosebud before you," and Ginger had brought her grandmother's debutante gown out of the storage closet.

Deena still hadn't agreed to let her wear it for her own debut—her mother treated it like some museum piece that should be preserved in a humidity-controlled Plexiglas box—but Ginger had her heart set on it.

They had nine months to go until the deb ball anyway. Invitations hadn't even gone out, though they'd be hand-delivered in a few days. Ginger couldn't imagine she wouldn't be a cinch to make the cut. Her grandmother, Rose Dupree, was one of the original Glass Slipper Club Rosebuds, and

Deena Dupree Fore had followed in her footsteps. It stood to reason that Ginger would be next.

And both Mac and Laura had agreed that it would take a colossal tripping-up for Ginger to be blackballed. Though it seemed strange, considering her antiestablishment attitude, Ginger was actually looking forward to using her debutante status to do good. So many girls just wanted the attention, wanted their names mentioned in the society column and in the glossy city magazines. For Ginger, it would be more than the "dutiful legacy keeps family tradition" shtick. It was all about philanthropy and aiming the spotlight at things that mattered.

And then there was the all-important matter of donning the perfect dress, even if it wasn't made of hemp.

"Okay, Laura, I quit. Get me out of this." Ginger's armpits felt damp beneath the layers of silk and the corset-like stays and what felt like a half-ton of petticoats rustling against her thighs. "If I get sweat stains on this thing, Deena's going to freak." Ginger ran a hand over the embroidered skirt. "Then I won't get to wear this, for sure."

"Dum-dum-duh-dum." Mac put aside her book and hummed a bit from Wagner's "Bridal Chorus." "You could always save it for your wedding, after you go on the Nicole Richie starvation diet."

"Very funny." Ginger tried to look over her shoulder. "C'mon, hurry up. I'm going to suffocate in, like, five seconds."

"I'm moving as fast as I can, considering my fingertips are completely numb." Laura hovered behind her, each button she unfastened allowing Ginger to take a slightly deeper breath.

Ginger put her hands on her belly, wishing she hadn't

eaten so much pizza. Between the champagne and the food, she wasn't feeling all that great. "I think I need to lie down," she said. "Or throw up."

"Can you hold that thought . . . wait, wait, *there*! You're free!" Laura said, helping Ginger step out of the ornate gown and the petticoats beneath it. "Face it, girl, you can't wear this sucker at our debut unless you have it altered."

"Altered?" Ginger froze, the yards and yards of white material gathered up in her arms. The face that looked back at her in the mirror had blanched so her freckles stood out like connect-the-dots on her nose and cheeks. "Deena would never let any of these seams be ripped out. She'll insist on new couture."

"I know you like recycling old things and I actually hate to agree with your mother, but maybe you should have a gown designed for you. It's not like your daddy can't afford it," Laura remarked, stepping up beside Ginger and looking over her own reflection. "I'm having Vera Wang do mine." She turned sideways and lifted her chin, studying her posture. "If anyone can make me look like Petra Nemcova, she can."

"You have your mother's gloves, don't you?"

Laura blushed like she'd done something naughty. "Oh, yeah, the gloves. They're the only part of Tincy's cotillion leftovers I can fit into."

"But you understand, then, about the history of something worn again," Ginger said, because her grandmother's dress and her own debut seemed undeniably linked. "It'll mean so much more sentimentally. Besides, buying new would be such a waste of money. Do you know how much a couture gown costs? That could feed, like, thousands of children in the Sudan."

"I'm just saying," Laura muttered. "And it's not like Daddy Fore couldn't afford Anna Sui or Stella McCartney or Versace, for that matter," she added under her breath as she left Ginger's side and walked toward the bed. She plunked down beside Mac, giving the brunette a nudge. "So who's doing your dress, chica? And God help you if your stepmom's involved. She's a walking *Glamour* 'don't.' "

Mac got uncharacteristically quiet.

"Don't tell me she forced you into one of those slinky beauty-queen gowns with rhinestones and glitter," Laura joked.

"No, I won't be wearing a rhinestone dress," Mac said in a voice that was barely audible. "I'm not sure I'll be wearing a dress at all."

"So you're debuting naked, is that it?" Laura egged her on.

"Maybe I won't be debuting."

"What?"

Ginger draped her grandmother's gown across a chaise, leaving the petticoats in a pile on the floor. Something was clearly up with Mac, and Ginger had a good guess what it was. She padded over to the bed in her sweaty camisole and boxers, and she squeezed in between Laura and Mac, slinging an arm around Mac's shoulders.

"Hey, what's going on, Mackenzie? Don't tell me you're still undecided about accepting a Rosebud invitation. I thought we'd all made a pact to go through it together. We're the Three Amigas, right?"

Mac squirmed, and Ginger read the uncertainty in her face. The pale eyes behind the glasses glanced away.

"I'm just not sure it's what I want," she mumbled.

Laura blurted out, "You can't be serious! God, it's going to be the greatest party of all time, better than sex." She hesitated. "No, scratch that. Make that better than chocolate. Can't you picture it?" Laura got off the bed and held her arm up, as if she were walking into the room with an escort. "You're all dolled up as you step into the ballroom on your dad's elbow, and they announce for all the world to hear, 'Miss Michelle Jeanette Mackenzie, daughter of Daniel Mackenzie and—' "

Laura stopped and dropped her arm, flushing with embarrassment. "Oh, damn, I'm sorry. I wasn't thinking."

"How they would announce me when my mother's dead, you mean?" Mac's voice sounded raspy. "Daughter of Daniel and the late Jeanie Mackenzie, stepdaughter of the totally irritating Honey Potts?" Her slim shoulders shuddered. "It's bad enough that my mom won't be there, but the stepmonster has already assured me she'll be watching every step of the way. She got Daddy to freaking *buy* her a seat on the GSC selection committee."

"No way," Ginger gasped. "But that's good, right? She'll make sure your bid isn't blocked."

"It feels a little like a lie, like I'll have to pretend to be someone I'm not, and I don't know if I can go through with it."

Ginger caught the glisten of tears in her friend's eyes and squeezed her arm.

"But, sweetie, you know it's what your mom wanted. You've told us a million times about the letters she left you."

Laura jumped in before Mac could so much as reply, "How could you even think of declining when you're a lock? I want this so bad I can taste it, and I'm not even sure I'm getting in, despite everything Tincy's done. And if I don't get it, if they decide I don't look the part, I'm screwed. And Jo Lynn Bidwell will have the last laugh. Damn, it just can't happen like that. It can't." She put her hands on her hips and shook her head, looking both scared and pissed. "I'm still trying to figure out what third-world country I'll have to move to if they pass me over. Mozambique? Tunisia? Burundi? Where is Burundi, anyway?"

Man, Ginger mused, *Laura sure has it in for Jo Lynn.* Whatever that snob had done to Laura around the time she and Avery had broken up must've burned. Laura had returned to the fold without saying a word except that she didn't want to talk about it. *Ever.* And she'd never mentioned it since. Sometimes Laura's life looked like a soap opera in real time, with Laura playing the self-absorbed ingénue. Much as Ginger loved the girl, she could do with a little less drama.

"If I were you—" Laura started in on Mac again only to get cut off midsentence.

"But I'm not *you,*" Mac said, "and what if being a Rosebud isn't me?"

"Please." Laura laughed, but there wasn't a drop of humor in the sound. "You're such a Honda, I swear."

"A Honda?" Ginger repeated, squishing up her forehead. "What?"

"It was a quiz in *Cosmo* that I read on the plane," Laura explained. " *'Are U Your Car?'* I'm definitely a Mercedes Roadster, sexy and young and ready for anything," she said, throwing up her arms and shaking her booty to demonstrate. "You, Ging, you're a Prius, no question. Concerned about the world around you and not so concerned about designer tags. On the other hand, there's our oh-so-grounded Mackenzie." Laura wagged a finger at the brunette. "She's the total Honda Civic. Practical, responsible, and as far from spontaneous as you can get."

Mac stiffened.

"Laura," Ginger said, wondering what the hell was going on with her friend. Laura was being a total jerk and completely insensitive.

"What?" Laura blinked. "It's the truth, isn't it? Tell me it's not."

"It's okay," Mac said quietly, but Ginger could sense that it was far from it.

Crap, my sleepover is turning into a nightmare, and it's only half-past nine!

"Maybe we should talk about something else," she suggested.

"Something besides Rosebud invitations? Are y'all crazy? What else is there worth discussin' except guys, and you'll jump on me like a pack of wolves if I even mention Avery."

That wasn't exactly the change in conversation Ginger had hoped for.

Laura sighed and glanced at the Patek Philippe sparkling on her wrist. "Oh, hell, it's almost ten o'clock. I've gotta go out for a bit, but I'll be back, okay? Ginger, can I borrow your house key?" She looked around, spotted what she wanted, and scooped up the key chain from the dresser before Ginger could open her mouth. "All right, then, I'm off. Leave a light on for me."

Ginger glared at Laura's departing back but let her go without a word. *How rude to just walk out like that!* Did Laura mean to spoil their last sleepover of the summer? Heck, the only sleepover they'd had in months. Ginger wondered what had gotten into her and figured it had to be Mr. Football. It was like a full moon every night when Avery Dorman came sniffing around.

With a sigh, Ginger turned to Mac and asked, "Are you okay?"

"I'm fine, really." Mac summoned up a closemouthed smile. "What the heck was that about anyway?"

"Who knows," Ginger replied—not exactly the truth. Somehow she knew Laura's irrational behavior had everything to do with Avery. And, like she'd told Mac earlier, you couldn't rationalize sex, not any more than you could turn a Mercedes Roadster into something more practical.

The devil and I
certainly had one thing in common:
we were both horny.
——Dolly Parton

Absence might make the heart grow fonder,
but *abstinence* can drive a girl to drink.
——Jo Lynn Bidwell

Eight

Jo Lynn loved that it was so easy to party, despite the fact that living in the burbs in a sprawling city like Houston sometimes put a crimp in *where* the party happened. The city was too big to navigate quickly or easily. Depending on time of day, traffic, and, God forbid, construction, it could take *forever* to get downtown when you lived outside the Loop. Even hitting the bars in Rice Village near the university could be a real pain in the ass, unless fate was smiling on you and everyone else stayed off the road that night.

The less-demanding crowd hung out at Jamba Juice or Chipotle, met at bowling alleys or the movies, gathered at the Galleria, or cruised Westheimer looking for playmates, while the kickers in their Tony Lamas and Stetsons line danced at Midnight Rodeo in Katy.

Jo Lynn and her crew weren't into any of that.

If they were feeling adventurous, they made their way to the downtown clubs, like the M Bar on Main Street with its soft lights, Oriental rugs, and potted palms, or Next in the Warehouse District with its metallic deejay booth and Plexiglas dance cage. Dressed like divas with perfect hair and polished makeup, they always made it past the bouncers with ease. But mostly they stayed home and played at who-ever's house was empty that weekend. All her peeps had parents who traveled extensively, often for a month at a time, soaking up the sun at their villas on the Riviera or their beach houses in Costa Rica, or escaping the heat at their cabins in Telluride or Beaver Creek, always leaving their liquor cabinets well stocked and their fridges full of munchies. The house staff obligingly turned a blind eye if the mice wanted to play while the cats were away. And nobody said a word.

Tonight was Jo's turn to play hostess since her folks were conveniently away. She was having a very private little shindig in the guesthouse for her closest friends—and the hottest guys—so that they could mourn the passing of summer.

The Bidwell manse had been left in the care of the family's ancient housekeeper, Nan, who could barely keep her eyes open past ten. Just in case, Jo Lynn had given Nan a bottle of 1997 Beringer Bancroft Ranch merlot from her father's wine cellar and had sent her off to her room at eight, knowing Nan would drink every drop and be out like a light by the time Jo's buds started arriving.

She had the guesthouse all ready: she'd lit at least a dozen candles, put out her iPod stereo with its cute iWoofer speakers, and set out bowls and bowls of fresh chips and salsa from Pappasito's. She had all the ingredients to whip up the perfect icy margaritas, including several bottles of her daddy's primo Patrón.

Dillon adored a good margarita. And Jo Lynn aimed to get him good and drunk. It was part of her plan to put Dillon in the mood for love.

Like the Girl Scout she'd never been, Jo Lynn Bidwell was always prepared. She had on her sexiest black lace push-up La Perla bra and matching thong to ensure she'd need the Trojans she'd tucked in the drawer of the nightstand beside the king-sized bed in the largest of the guesthouse bedrooms.

She heard the iPod segue from the All-American Rejects to Boys Like Girls, and she felt a prickle of anticipation, the hairs tingling at the back of her neck.

Was it nearly time to rock and roll?

She glanced at her Rolex; its diamond-studded face showed she had five minutes before Trisha and Camie arrived. The guys were due to come ten or fifteen minutes after. That was how it always worked.

Jo checked her makeup in the bathroom mirror, smudging the lines below her deep-blue eyes just a smidge more so they'd look smoky and sexy. Her MAC shadow, in a shade called Shroom, set off her tanned skin, as did the pale and sweet Stila lip glaze. Her perfectly highlighted hair had been dried straight and hung like shiny gold curtains on either side of her heart-shaped face.

How could Dillon resist?

Jo Lynn stared at her own reflection, smoothing the front of her clingy black sundress, noting how small it made the curve of her waist look between her perfectly balanced D cups and her slim hips.

People often told her she looked like Reese Witherspoon, only taller, prettier, and with a much nicer rack. Her appearance had gotten her more than attention in her seventeen years. It had won her more trophies, scholarship money, sashes, and sparkly tiaras than she knew what to do with.

Bootsie, the stage mother to beat all stage mothers, had turned the least-used of the Bidwell mansion's six bedrooms into a shrine to Jo's pageant career.

But that part of her life was dead and buried, as far as Jo Lynn was concerned.

Being a debutante would be so different. Pageants were all about the sparkle and glitter, the song and dance, smiling till your cheeks ached and worrying every second whether your hair was out of place, whether you'd trip on your sequined gown going down the steps, and whether you'd used enough boob tape. Jo Lynn no longer wanted to play princess for a day, wearing a rhinestone crown and waving to the crowd. She yearned for something more than a title or scholarship money she didn't need. The world she aimed to compete in was ruled by power and bloodlines, not big hair and tap-dance routines. She knew that the best way to gain entrée to the people who mattered most in Houston was being named a Glass Slipper Club deb. Every woman who'd ever been selected had gone on to greater things, and Jo Lynn intended to do the same.

She had the next stage of her life planned out in three neat steps, and she kept the handwritten list tucked under her pillow. That way, she'd be sure to dream about everything on it when she fell asleep each night.

★ *Become a Glass Slipper Club debutante*
★ *Go to whatever Texas college Dillon signs with*
★ *Marry Dillon and have his babies*

Jo Lynn was nothing if not focused.

And her focus tonight was solely on getting physical with Dillon. Two weeks without sex was way too long, and the pressure was starting to get to her.

Why hadn't he wanted to get busy lately? Was he as distracted as he claimed? Or was he just not attracted to her anymore, not the way that he had been before, anyway?

The idea that he might be tiring of her made her crazy. She and Dillon had been together for two years, ever since she'd broken up with Avery to be with him. Jo wondered if they'd gotten too comfortable together, if she just didn't do it for him anymore. *Oh, God, please don't let it be that!* she thought, and took a deep breath, telling herself that she couldn't freak out tonight, couldn't break down and cry, even if she wanted to. She had to stay cool and calm, make Dillon think everything was all right, and she could only think of one way to do it.

She ripped open her Hermès croc clutch and rummaged for the slim brown bottle with her mother's name on it. She struggled with the lid before getting it open and shaking out two tiny white pills. She made a face as she placed them on her tongue, hating the bitter taste. Quickly, she turned on the faucet and cupped a handful of water, enough to swallow the Xanax in one gulp.

There, Jo told herself. *All better.*

Within minutes, she felt a familiar calm easing through her veins. She hated to resort to Mommy's Little Helpers, but this was an emergency. She had to be relaxed and ready for whatever was to come (and, hopefully, that would mean Dillon).

Hello, gorgeous, she could hear him saying, and she closed her eyes, imagining his hands on her skin, his fingers untying her halter dress and gently tugging it down. . . .

"Yoo-hoo! It's me and Trisha. Where ya hidin', girlfriend?"

Jo Lynn jumped, her eyes popping open. She hadn't even heard anyone come through the front door to the guest-house.

"Hey, Jo-L, where are you? The gang's all here!"

Well, part of the gang, anyway, Jo Lynn thought.

Camie's loud voice rang out from the living room, cutting through the wailing of The Killers' "Mr. Brightside" (which Jo Lynn took as a message: *look on the bright side*), so she quickly stashed the bottle in her purse, pasting a picture-perfect smile on her face as she emerged from the bathroom to greet her friends.

"Hey, y'all!" she said, flinging her arms wide and exchanging air kisses.

Then she gushed over how great each looked: Camie with her dark hair piled in a loose knot on her head, her tanned skin glowing against the white of her tiny Versace minidress, and Trisha with her red-gold hair flipped up where it just grazed her shoulders, wearing the loudest Pucci sundress Jo Lynn had ever seen.

"You got the 'ritas mixed?" Camie asked, making her way around the granite breakfast bar into the kitchen. " 'Cuz I'm ready to get this party going."

"The guys won't be here for a few minutes," Jo Lynn said.

"They'll have to catch up, then." Camie was already toss-ing stuff into the blender, and she turned the noisy thing on before Jo Lynn could even protest.

"Make one for me," Trisha hollered before heading in the opposite direction. She dropped her purse next to the L-shaped sectional sofa with its huge down-filled cushions, arranged around a sixty-inch plasma TV. She turned the set on but kept the sound off and began flipping wildly from channel to channel while the All-American Rejects sang "Dirty Little Secret."

"Dirty little secret? How appropriate," Cam said after she'd turned off the blender and was filling the oversized margarita glasses Jo Lynn had set out. "I happen to have some dirt to share."

"About who?" Jo Lynn asked, though she really didn't care. She only had one thing on her mind tonight, and it was six feet two inches with blue eyes and sandy blond hair.

"That slut Jessica Rembert." Camie's eyes widened with glee. "Someone caught her drunk out on the town in a dress prone to nip slips and minus her panties. There are, like, six pics up on some Caldwell dude's Facebook page. They're obviously shot with a cell phone, but they're clear enough that it'll keep her off the Rosebud list, thank God."

"Like that ho even had a shot." Jo Lynn sniffed. "Bootsie would rip my head off if I ever did anything that stupid."

Besides, she knew better.

Plenty of pageant girls didn't wear panties, but that was a different story entirely. Panty lines were a no-no, and any beauty queen worth her sash had a suitcase full of hose with cotton crotches. As a matter of fact, everyone on the pageant circuit knew how to exit a limo without flashing the world. It was, like, the second thing they taught you, after how to walk down stairs in four-inch heels without falling on your ass.

"Here's your 'rita," Camie said, handing Jo Lynn a glass. "And yours, Trish, get over here, girl!"

Like an overeager puppy, Trisha leapt off the couch and bounded across the room, accepting the proffered drink and wasting no time in noisily sucking on the red and white striped cocktail straw. When she came up for air, she tucked a red-gold strand of hair behind her ear and asked, "What were y'all talking about?"

"Dirt," Jo Lynn said, sipping her drink and gazing at the door, thinking that any minute Dillon would walk in.

"About Laura Bell?" Trish asked.

"No, Jessica Rembert." Camie set down her empty margarita glass. "Why? Do you know something about the Hostess Cupcake?" She leaned over the counter toward her friend. "What'd you hear?"

"Okay, okay." Trisha seemed breathless before she even started to explain. "Suzy Bacino heard from Danielle Bartlett, who flew home on Southwest after visiting her cousin in El Paso, or some other god-awful place, that Avery Dorman showed up at Hobby Airport and picked up Laura on her way home from fat camp!"

"What?" Camie blinked, her tanned face suddenly ashen.

"Supposedly, he snatched her away, right under the nose of her two best buddies, Green Girl and Bookworm." Trisha's voice dripped sarcasm.

Jo Lynn heard the names Laura Bell and Avery Dorman and stopped staring at the door, intrigued enough to pay attention.

"That's totally messed up." Camie looked sick. "Why would he do that?"

"Sorry, Cam, I know you like the dude and y'all had a thing going earlier this summer, but it sounds like he's slumming again," Trish assured her. "Suzy says Danielle's completely reliable. Besides, that burnt orange 'Vette is hard to miss."

"Oops," Jo Lynn said, putting a hand to her mouth. "I guess I shouldn't have invited him tonight, then, huh?"

"Avery's coming here? After he hooked up with Laura Bell?" Camie knocked her glass over, the dregs of her margarita oozing onto the granite countertop, and she backed away, careful not to get any on her white dress. "Are you trippin', Jo-L?"

"Sorry, I had no clue." Jo Lynn apologized without really meaning it. She had to admit she got a kick out of the fact that she had a certain sway over Avery, especially when it came to the girls he dated. And maybe Jo Lynn did still feel the teensiest bit possessive of Avery, not that *she* ever wanted him again, not that way . . . not after how quickly he'd rebounded from her to Laura Bell, just to rub her nose in it. She and Avery were a lot alike, that was all: two very pretty peas in a pod who hadn't worked out together. Jo Lynn's heart belonged to Dillon.

"He's not bringing Laura's fat ass *with* him, is he?" Cam asked pointedly.

"He'd better not." Or Jo Lynn would be as pissed off as Camie. "You want me to have Dillon toss him out when he gets here?"

Camie opened her mouth, fit to burst, and Jo Lynn expected to hear a "Hell, yes!"

But, strangely, Camie closed her trap and gnawed on her lip for a second before asking, "Did you say Dillon was bringing Mike and Brody with him?"

"Yes."

"Hmm, Mike's hot enough, I guess." Camie set her hands on her hips, her chin lifted defiantly. "Maybe I'll just give Avery a bit of his own medicine."

Jo Lynn smiled at her and reached out to pat her hand. "That's my girl."

"We've got to make sure that debu-tank doesn't end up on the Rosebud list, Jo-L," Camie begged. "I don't care that her mother's in the GSC and was a Rosebud, Laura's a lowlife."

"Well, it's not surprising, is it?" Trish interjected. "Her daddy sells sewers."

"More like plumbing parts," Jo Lynn corrected.

"Okay, toilets, then. Whatev." Trisha rolled her eyes and went back to the television.

Camie headed over to the blender, banging around as she mixed another batch of margaritas, calling out over the noisy whir, "Hey, y'all, how 'bout seconds?"

But Jo Lynn ignored her. Her ears had picked up the sound of a car pulling into the drive, the low rumble of the motor sounding exactly like the purr of Dillon's black Mustang convertible.

She smoothed her halter dress and wet her lips, a prickle of anticipation racing across her skin as she caught the slam of car doors outside, then a quick knock before Dillon let himself in.

"Hey, sounds like a party's goin' on in here," he said as he entered with Mike and Brody right behind him.

Brody paused at the door, holding it open and giving a sharp whistle, before a black lab with its leash dragging galloped into the guesthouse and raced toward Jo Lynn, wagging its tail and sticking its nose right in her crotch.

Lovely.

Dillon observed with his arms crossed over his broad chest, an amused look on his handsome face.

Jo pushed its head away, saying, "Nice doggy," as it slobbered all over her hand before it took off, sniffing various points around the room until Brody caught its dangling leash and led it outside. Through the French doors, Jo Lynn saw him tug the dog around the unscreened porch and tie it to the railing. As soon as Dillon's buddy had stepped back inside, she drawled, "For heaven's sake, Brody, you weren't supposed to bring a date."

Brody shrugged his linebacker's shoulders and scratched at the stubble on his square chin. "It's my dad's hunting dog, Bubba. He's a great birder, but his manners leave a lot to be desired. I'm watching him this weekend while they're in Palm Springs—"

"How interesting," Jo Lynn cut him off before her eyes could glaze over. Brody was pretty much a Bubba himself, always wearing cowboy boots and dipping chaw. *Yuck.* If he spat in anything tonight except a plastic cup, she'd throw his ass out on the porch with his dog. "I'm sure Trish will be glad she doesn't have to share you tonight," she remarked, having to shout over the music as Mike turned up the iPod and Nelly Furtado's "Promiscuous" filled the room with its sexy beat.

As soon as Jo Lynn sidestepped the six-foot-four, 240-pound Brody, Trisha stuck to him like Velcro, taking his hand and leading him over to the sofa. Within a blink, the strawberry blonde was in his lap and they were kissing.

Like the animals on Noah's ark, her party guests quickly paired up.

Camie wasted no time in heading Mike's way with two fresh margaritas, one of which he held in one hand as he did a bad impression of dirty dancing while Camie drank and giggled. A few stragglers, like Avery and a couple of other Caldwell guys, would no doubt show up later. But Jo Lynn didn't care. She stood still, the noise swirling around her, her gaze fixated on Dillon in his tight polo and jeans as he came toward her.

"Hey, babe," he said, and gave her a perfunctory kiss on the forehead. "You got a drink for me?"

"I'll make yours special," she told him, her heart pounding as she thought about how much tonight meant for them. It was hard as hell for her to be around him anymore without wanting him so badly it hurt; she couldn't stand too much more rejection.

Dillon's gaze followed her as she moved around the tiny kitchen, and she hoped he didn't notice how nervous she was. She banged bottles together and dropped crushed ice on the floor as she threw together their margaritas, adding twice as much Patrón as she normally did.

"They'll be ready in a sec," she told him, leaning in so he could hear her over the music and the blender. She took hold of his arm, curling her fingers around the taut muscles, inhaling the scent of him, clean like soap with just a hint of citrus cologne.

"You look great," he told her, his lips brushing her ear, and Jo Lynn felt the warmth that spread through her lower belly.

"You do too," she said, laying her palm against his cheek. She hated to let go of him.

As soon as the margaritas were mixed, she shut the blender off and poured him a heaping glass, giving herself far less. The drinks were perfect: frothy and cold with no salt on the rims, just the way Dillon liked them.

A few other friends dropped by, making themselves at home, raiding the fridge for beer and wine coolers or drinking the Patrón straight out of the bottle. But Jo Lynn hardly noticed they were there, not once Dillon had slurped down several potent 'ritas and was nibbling on her ear.

"C'mon," she said, tugging him up from the leather armchair they'd been curled up on. "I've got something to show you."

He was a little unsteady on his feet, but willing enough so that she led him away from the main scene and down the hallway to the empty master bedroom. Once she'd nudged him through the door and locked it closed behind them, she drew him toward the bed and gave him a gentle push down onto the mattress.

"So what'd you wan' me ta see?" he asked her, sounding about one drink shy of passing out.

"This," Jo Lynn said, and untied her halter dress, dropping it to her feet and standing before him in nothing but her lacy push-up bra and thong.

"Well, damn," she heard Dillon say, before she walked up to the bed and straddled him. Her hips pressed against his pelvis as she kissed him, her hair falling in curtains around their faces. She tasted the sweetness of the tequila on his lips and on his teeth as he opened his mouth to her, and their tongues did a familiar dance, the world slipping away. . . .

"Jo, hey, whoa," he said, his voice soft and slurred. He turned his face briefly away, but she didn't stop.

Instead, she ran her lips along his jaw, then down his neck to the collar of his polo. "Off," she breathed, grabbing the material, pulling it up until he raised his arms and ducked his head and she ripped it off as fast as she was able.

She pressed her face against his chest, her fingers sliding over the sculpted muscles, her tongue tracing a path from his sternum along the baby-soft hairs to his belly-button and then to the waist of his jeans. Her hand reached for the metal buttons and started working them free.

"Jo, c'mon," he said again, more insistently, and she hesitated long enough to look up into his face, his expression panicked.

"I know it's been two weeks since we, you know," she whispered, "but it's like ridin' a bike. You never forget."

"Babe, I wish I could, but I can't—" He tried to sit up, but she leaned her weight forward, her palms on his chest, pushing him back down.

She was not about to give up so easily.

"Sure you can, darlin'. I'll help you." She was nose to nose with him, staring into the eyes she loved so much, the blue almost indigo in the dark. "Besides, it's not like I don't love you and you don't love me back, right?"

His Adam's apple did a bob as he swallowed before nodding. "Yeah, of course."

"Then what're we waiting for?" She smiled at him, feeling his quickened heartbeat slam against his chest, nearly in time with her own. "I need you so much, Dill. I've missed you so much I could die."

"I'm so sorry," he said hoarsely, and she saw tears on his lashes.

He missed her too, she knew. *What else could it be?*

She began to peel down his jeans, exposing paisley boxers, and she lowered her head, her pink lips parting as, from the pocket of Dillon's jeans, the Caldwell Fight Song started playing.

What the f—?

Dillon moaned and pushed her away as he scrambled to

get up and reach for his pants, but Jo Lynn had her hand in his pocket before he could get to it.

She flipped the phone open and was about to answer to find out who it was when Dillon snatched his cell from her hand, glanced at the screen, flipped it shut, and shoved it back in his pocket.

"I'd better go," he mumbled as he tugged his jeans back up and buttoned them in haste, glancing around for his shirt while Jo Lynn helplessly watched him.

"You're leaving?" She folded her arms over her breasts.

"Have to," he grunted.

"Is it an emergency?"

"Something like that, yeah."

He put on his shirt and flip-flops, then stumbled toward the door.

Jo Lynn didn't know what the hell was going on, but Bootsie hadn't trained her for situations like this. Jo Lynn could set a table with all the forks and spoons in the right place. She could strut across a stage in a floor-length gown and four-inch heels with blinding lights in her eyes and not miss a beat. But how was she supposed to handle her boyfriend walking out on her in the middle of seducing him?

"You okay to drive?" she asked, because he couldn't seem to walk a straight line, and Dillon never got behind the wheel when he'd had one too many. He'd always stay in bed with her until he'd sobered up in the morning. It had always been that way.

"I'm okay."

"Call me?"

"I will."

"I love you," she told him, in lieu of goodbye.

He paused, glancing back at where she stood, nearly naked and alone in the middle of the room. Then he unlocked the door and was gone.

Jo Lynn shivered and rubbed her arms. Part of her wanted to rush after him and beg him to stay, but girls like her didn't chase after boys. It was always the other way around.

So she let him go, pulled on her dress, and returned to the party alone.

Sex is part of nature.
I go along with nature.
——Marilyn Monroe

When you love someone,
no matter how smart you are,
how tough you claim to be,
or how burned you've been,
it's impossible to say no.
——Laura Bell

Nine

Laura parked her cherry red Mercedes at the very end of the private lane where the Bidwells lived.

"Avery, you'd better be here," she murmured, glancing around in the dark at the thick clusters of trees. Their outstretched branches seemed to reach toward her like monstrous arms as they swayed in the lukewarm breeze.

Sighing, she trudged through the dark, her high-heeled satin Christian Louboutin sandals clicking noisily on the asphalt. Twice she had to stop to pick gravel out from between her toes, but it was worth it, not getting too close to the main house or the guesthouse, where Avery said the party would be going on.

Avery definitely seemed to be testing her, practically daring her to stand up to Jo Lynn, which was an interesting twist. Laura had always been up-front with Avery about her feelings for him. *He* was the one who should be walking through fire. Not that Laura hadn't dreamed of facing off with Jo Lynn Bidwell and clawing her eyes out someday—hell, the witch deserved a lot worse for what she'd done.

But with debutante invitations going out in mere days, Laura would rather avoid a scene and not risk having Jo

Lynn tear the scab off old wounds. If she and the Queen Bee got into a catfight, Bootsie Bidwell would undoubtedly catch wind of it by morning. And the one thing Laura didn't need right now was having the chair of the Rosebud selection committee pissed off at her before D-Day. That would be deb suicide. Laura realized she was on the bubble as it was, and she couldn't afford to blow it.

Tiny solar lights lined the long driveway of the Bidwells' sprawling manor, and Laura veered to the right, following the path around the house. She heard music and raucous laughter before she glimpsed the guesthouse. Unlike the darkened main house, the windows winked with light, as did the huge oval-shaped pool alongside it. The water glowed a brilliant blue, the surface smooth and still.

Guess no one wanted to dive in. Like Jo Lynn and her Bimbo Cartel would risk getting their hair wet, Laura thought with a smirk, knowing their habits well enough. She'd been part of the group while she and Avery had dated, so she realized how things went. When you had Jo Lynn's stamp of approval, everything was golden. If Jo Lynn got tired of you or thought you were taking up too much of her spotlight, she could turn on you in the blink of an eye. That was what had happened to Laura, though Laura wasn't sure which reason applied.

If she took a guess, she figured it had to do with Avery's history with Jo Lynn. Laura knew he was Jo Lynn's first, and the Queen of Mean still acted like she owned him, even though she was supposedly head over heels in love with Dillon Masters. Laura imagined Jo-L wasn't too keen on the idea of Avery being with a girl who wasn't a perfect size two, like it somehow dissed her. Or maybe there was more to it than that, some deep dark secret between Jo Lynn and Avery. If that was the case, Laura had no clue what the secret was. Avery would never answer when she asked.

Oh, well, she told herself. Tonight wasn't about the bad old days—it was about the here and now. So far as Laura was concerned, Avery was her present and future, and nothing Jo Lynn could do anymore would affect that.

Nearly a dozen cars were parked along the drive, and Laura smiled with relief when she spotted Avery's Corvette. He was here, somewhere. She just had to find him without running into Jo-L.

Laura jumped at the noise of a screen door slapping closed, and she realized someone had emerged from the cottage. A tall guy stumbled down the steps, heading toward her with his head down, talking on his cell in low tones.

Is that Dillon Masters? Oh, God! He was coming her way! If he saw her and told Jo Lynn she was here, all hell would break loose.

As Laura was making a beeline for the nearest hiding place, Dillon dropped his keys. They hit the stone path with a clatter, and he bent clumsily to retrieve them. That gave her time to slip behind a thick tree. She pressed her hands against the rough bark as she waited for Dillon to leave.

When he climbed into his Mustang and drove off with a screech of wheels, Laura let out a breath. She removed her sandals, catching the straps around her fingers, before she tiptoed toward the guesthouse, the short grass tickling the soles of her feet as she headed toward the shrubs beneath a large unshuttered window.

The sound of Big and Rich thumped against the night air, telling everybody to save a horse and ride a cowboy.

Laura lifted her head carefully, peering through the glass and quickly taking in the scene. A large collection of empty beer and wine cooler bottles littered a coffee table. That was a boatload of booze for such a small crowd. She counted eight people in all, and none of them was Avery.

Damn it, where is he?

Clutching her Louboutins in one hand, she picked her way around the guesthouse, ducking below windows and following the carved wooden railing. As she neared the front French doors, a large black shadow rose from the porch floor and lunged at her, barking wildly. Laura yelped, her pulse skyrocketing as she backed away from the creature, trying hard not to trip over her own feet.

That was it. She'd had it.

Avery could rot in hell—yet again—for playing games with her.

She turned around, heading for the steps down to the lawn, aiming to run all the way back to her car in her bare feet before she got caught.

Just as her feet touched grass, a hand snagged her arm, preventing her from going anywhere. Her shoes fell from her grasp, and she opened her mouth to yell, but a second hand clamped across her face and smothered the sound.

"What're you tryin' to do? Wake the dead?" Avery drawled in her ear, waiting until the coast was clear to release her.

"Me? What were *you* tryin' to do? Play hide-and-seek? How on earth was I supposed to find you?" Laura smelled beer on his breath, maybe even a hint of pot smoke clinging to his hair and clothes. "You jerk!" She pushed hard at his chest, and he stumbled back against the hedge. "I should've stayed at Ginger's house. I must be out of my mind."

"Ouch," he said, plucking a twig from his hair and following her as she strode away from him.

Laura didn't realize she'd headed toward the pool until she was standing on the cool tiles that wrapped around the pale blue oval. If she'd been at home or even at Ginger's house, she would've been tempted to strip down to her panties and bra and jump in. The air was still sticky, and she was definitely "glowing," as Tincy Bell delicately referred to sweating like a pig, especially after her trek from the car and after that huge dog had nearly scared the pee out of her.

"Listen, I wasn't even inside with the rest of them. I was sitting there," Avery said, coming up beside her and pointing to a vacant chaise with a rumpled beach towel and three empty Spaten bottles beside it. "I was wondering where you were and wishing you'd hurry up so I could do a little of this"—he reached for her, catching her fingers in his—"and a lot of this." His mouth came down gently on hers as he kissed her.

Oh, my.

Laura's shoes fell to the patio, and she wrapped her arms around his neck, kissing him like she hadn't seen him in a year. Even though she hadn't had a lick of booze, she felt intoxicated, all dizzy and light-headed, as the touch of their lips eased from gentle to rougher, his tongue sliding past her teeth, teasing.

"What the hell do you think you're doing?"

The angry voice cut through the night like a knife, and it jerked Laura out of Avery's embrace, the spell shattered.

She quickly stepped away from him, wiping her mouth with the back of her hand, and turned to find Jo Lynn Bidwell, flanked by her cronies, Camie and Trisha, standing not four feet away, their fists set squarely on their skinny hips.

"My, my, my, look who it is," Jo Lynn drawled, and the venomous tone made Laura's insides start to crumble. "If it isn't Laura Bell, fresh out of fat camp. Who invited you, Swamp Donkey? Because it wasn't *me* and this is *my* party. You're not wanted here now any more than you were a year ago, so why don't you get out before you regret it."

"Yeah, get out, you piece of trash," Camie spat, while Trisha added, "You've got some balls, bitch."

Laura opened her mouth, but nothing came out other than "uhhh." This was exactly the scene she'd feared most, and it was unfolding right before her eyes. Visions flashed through her head, of a summer night much like this, of being too trusting and drinking way too much liquor, of passing out on the floor of the guesthouse and waking up the next morning to find–

Oh, God. She swallowed. She had to go, or Jo Lynn would do it again. She'd dig up the pictures.

"I–" Laura was starting to say, "I'm gone," feeling deflated, like all the wind had been knocked out of her. A familiar sick sensation filled her belly, and she wished she could close her eyes and disappear.

"Stop hassling Laura. She's here 'cuz I invited her," Avery said, stepping up beside her, and reached for Laura's hand. His skin felt so warm against hers, which had turned cold as ice. "So if you don't want her around, we'll both leave."

Laura nodded, biting her lip, relief gushing through her. Avery had actually stood up to Jo Lynn rather than quietly retreating. That took guts, more than most people had when it came to squaring off against the Bimbo Cartel.

Laura bent to gather up her shoes and heard Jo Lynn laugh.

"You can't be serious, Avery. What in God's name do you see in her?" Jo Lynn asked. "You can have any girl you want, and you'd settle for *that*? I mean, she's still got that *ginormous* ass."

"Oink oink," Camie kicked in, and Trisha followed suit.

Laura told herself to breathe, to ignore them, while the angry voice inside her head kept nagging, *Are you gonna let them push you around again? Let them take you down like this, in front of Avery?*

She straightened up slowly, her whole body trembling as the hatred she'd bottled up a year ago surged straight to the surface. She'd been nice until then, a good Texas belle, minding her manners and killing with kindness instead of going after Jo Lynn with a vengeance. In a blink, the good girl was gone.

"Screw you," Laura shouted at Jo Lynn, then turned on Camie and Trish. "Screw all of you!" If she'd been smart, she would've left, but she couldn't stop the hurt from boiling over. "Why don't you go back in your glass house and stop throwing stones, huh? Because I'd rather have a big ass than a boyfriend who can't stand to stay over on a Saturday night."

The oinking stopped, and Jo Lynn stared at her, slack-jawed and bug-eyed. "What did you just say?"

"I *said* that I saw Dillon leaving, all hot and heavy on his cell like he had another date. What's that about, huh?" Laura threw out, emboldened, her adrenaline rushing too fast for her to stop and think about the consequences. "Has Big Dill stopped jonesing for you too, like every other guy does when he realizes you're as hollow inside as a cheap chocolate Easter bunny?"

Laura heard the collective gasp after she'd said it and the heat in her veins turned ice cold again.

"Whoa, this is getting out of hand," Avery whispered, and gave her a tug. "Let's go, Laura. *Now*."

"She's not going anywhere," Jo Lynn spat, her face the ugliest shade of purple Laura had ever seen. Then she charged at Laura like a bull, shrieking, *"Aaaaaaahhhh!"*

The force of Jo Lynn's body slamming into hers knocked Laura off her feet, and she felt herself falling backward into nothingness until her back slapped against the surface of the pool. Water splashed up around her before she started sinking, breathing bubbles up her nose.

She hit the bottom fast, and she realized she was at the shallow end. She quickly set her feet down and surfaced, gasping and sputtering.

Jo Lynn was flailing in the water beside her, screeching, "My hair, my hair!"

All that Laura could remember afterward were Avery's strong hands helping her up the steps and out of the water, and then him wrapping a dry beach towel around her before he carried her all the way to her car. He set her down gently, the asphalt of the road warm under her feet, and she leaned against the Mercedes, looking up at him, feeling her wet hair drip onto her shoulders.

"Are you crying?" he asked, brushing her cheeks with his thumb, but she shook her head.

"It's just pool water," she told him, a little white lie. She didn't want him to know how shaken up she was, how worried she was about what Jo Lynn and her crew might do in retaliation. "Really, I'll be okay."

"You sure?"

"Yeah." She tried to wring water out of the hem of her dress but quickly gave up, letting the material cling to her thighs. "I should be used to this by now, right? Pretty much the only way to completely avoid Jo Lynn Bidwell would be to leave town."

"She doesn't like you," Avery said matter-of-factly, and glanced over his shoulder, as if afraid Jo Lynn might come after them.

"Well, duh." Laura rolled her eyes. Like *that* wasn't stating the obvious!

"It's because she can't control you. You're just who you are. You don't care what anyone else thinks."

"You're wrong," she said, and put her hand on his chest, right over his heart. "I care what you think, Avery. Why can't you just *be* with me? Why does Jo Lynn even have to be in the picture? Has she got something on you? Because that's what it feels like."

Avery didn't speak for a long moment. Was it her imagination, or did he actually *flinch*?

He did that funny one-eyed squint guys seem to do when they're trying to come up with an answer that won't get them into trouble. "I wish I could explain," he finally said, "but I can't."

"Can't or *won't*?" Laura didn't get it.

"Maybe she's jealous," he offered softly.

"Of me?" Laura raised her eyebrows, incredulous. "Right." She laughed dryly. "Like I have anything she wants." And Jo-L sure seemed to make sure Laura didn't have Avery for long, whenever she did manage to "get" him for a while.

Avery met her eyes, and he wasn't smiling. She could tell he wasn't joking around. "Maybe you do and you don't even know it."

She stared at him, puzzled. If he didn't mean himself, what else was there? Could Jo Lynn Bidwell hate Laura for the mere fact that she liked who she was, no matter what size she wore, and that she had two best friends who loved her for who she was and not for what she could do for them? She opened her mouth to ask, but Avery spoke first.

"Look, I'd love to see you home . . . or back to Ginger's house . . . wherever you're going, but I need to go back and smooth things over." He shifted on his feet, clearly not comfortable. "I don't want this to turn into anything big. It's my fault for asking you to show up in the first place."

"It was *my* decision," Laura objected, not liking where their conversation was going. "You didn't force me to come."

"Didn't I?" he asked, and twisted a damp strand of hair around his finger before he let her go. "Drive safely, all right?"

"I will," Laura said, and felt like crying again, suddenly very tired. This night hadn't gone at all the way she'd hoped. In fact, it had ended pretty horribly.

Avery looked at her for a long moment, finally whispering goodbye before he turned away and picked up the sodden beach towel from the ground. He flung it over an arm and took off, loping back down the Bidwells' driveway.

Laura waited until she couldn't see him anymore, not even his shadow in the moonlight. *This night totally sucked,* she thought, and closed her eyes, letting out a slow breath as she yanked open the car door and got behind the wheel. She could barely function, operating by rote.

Somehow, she made it back to Ginger's house without running into a light pole or getting a ticket for speeding. She let herself in with Ginger's key, climbed the stairs, and walked into the bedroom.

Her two friends instantly stopped watching MTV, and their eyes bugged, no doubt a wee bit surprised to see she was drenched from head to toe, not to mention barefoot.

Before either could open her mouth to ask what happened, Laura held up a hand and said, "Don't ask."

And like the true BFFs they were, they didn't say another word.

There's not a game in the world you can play
without some risk of getting hurt.
—Katharine Hepburn

It's not true that I prefer books to boys.
They're just a lot easier to put down
when you need a break
and then pick up again
where you left off.
—Mac Mackenzie

Ten

As soon as she got home from Ginger's late on Sunday morning, Mac went straight upstairs and locked herself in her room. She put on her iPod and played Michael Bublé singing Sinatra at full blast while she danced around, shaking her hips and belting the lyrics into an imaginary microphone. Not that Mac was any good at singing *or* dancing, but it didn't matter. Like watching old black-and-white movies, listening to swing music relaxed her and made her forget whatever else was bugging her. And that was exactly what she needed right now.

When she had worn herself out, she sprawled across her bed, closing her eyes and catching her breath. She had to decompress after being over at Ginger's the night before. If that hadn't been the weirdest sleepover ever, it came awfully close. What the heck was wrong with Laura? Where had she gone last night and why wouldn't she spill?

One minute Ginger had been trying on her grandmother's ball gown on a dare, and the next, Laura had grabbed Ginger's house key and taken off after jumping all over Mac just because she was undecided about becoming a deb.

Mac didn't see what was so wrong with being confused about what she wanted, or with being a Honda Civic, for that matter. Just because Laura was obsessed with becoming a Rosebud—and Ginger, too, had embraced her deb destiny—it didn't mean that Mac felt the same way. If an invitation was hand-delivered to her door, and she decided to decline it, would that be the worst thing in the world? Would she be letting down her mother's memory *and* disappointing her two BFFs in one fell swoop?

Crud.

It was knowing her mother's wishes that made her choice so difficult. That was why seeing Ginger dressed up in Rose Dupree's white gown had been a little tough to take.

Jeanie Mackenzie had wanted Mac to don her gown too.

If you should want to wear the same dress I wore for my Rosebud Ball, I would love nothing more. Though I would understand if you chose to buy something new. Still, it would almost be as if I were there with you, Mackie, if you put on the de la Renta gown my mother watched me debut in. So think about it at the very least, would you? I would be so honored.

This wasn't going to be easy on her, was it? Not without her mom around, encouraging her, giving advice, and offering a shoulder to lean on when Mac needed it.

A lump settled in her throat, and Mac turned the music down, telling herself not to cry, that it would be okay. *Why am I still so emotional about things?* Two years without Jeanie Mackenzie around and she still couldn't get a grip sometimes. She just missed her mom so much. Mac closed her eyes, telling herself to just *breathe* until she felt calmer. Then she slid her journal out from beneath her pillow and sat cross-legged on her bed with the notebook in her lap. She tapped the pen against the page until she'd sorted out her thoughts. In a burst of frantic motion, she started scribbling down the words as fast as they came to her.

Sometimes I feel so alone, even if I'm in my house with my dad and Honey around, or with Ginger and Laura at a sleepover. I'm alone in a little shell that no one can penetrate. Every time I try to let something out, like how I feel about debuting, they don't seem to understand or take me seriously. It's like they want to impose their feelings on me, or they just ignore how I feel. Are they too afraid to deal with the deep, dark, unhappy aspects of my life? Like they have enough problems of their own, so they don't need to handle mine, too? Why can't I find someone who just listens and supports me? Who says, "It's okay if you don't want to be a Rosebud, Mac. You don't have to do it. Be yourself." Even if my mother were still alive, I'm not sure she'd understand why I'm conflicted any more than anyone else. I think she wanted me to be just like her, and that's not so bad. It's just that I'm a different person than she was. I'm Mac, not Jeanie.

She stopped writing, slipped the pen into the spine of her notebook, and closed the pages. Then she lay back against her pillows and sighed, going over way too many things in her head, like all the debutante crap, Laura hooking up with Avery again, and Ginger meeting up with this Javier dude tonight at the Sam Houston Oak. What had Ging said about that? Oh, yeah, that she was going to help stop the tree from being bulldozed to make room for more PFP parking.

Mac didn't like the sound of it but had promised to come up with a way to break Ging out of her grandmother's house before seven this evening. She had no clue yet how she was going to manage that without Ginger's mom and Rose Dupree, her grandma, figuring out that something was up.

Wait a minute, that was kind of spontaneous, wasn't it? And even if it wasn't, what was so wrong with being sensible? At least *she* wasn't going all soppy over a boy, like Laura over Avery. Mac knew he was going to blow Laura off again, like every time before. Did Avery have anything to do with Laura returning to Ginger's soaking wet? Mac figured he had to be responsible. That guy spelled trouble with a capital *T*, though Laura couldn't seem to see it through her rose-colored glasses.

Mac's cell rang, playing the overture from Mozart's *Figaro*. She grabbed it from her nightstand, reading Alex's number before she answered with a breathy "Hey!"

"You want to come over for lunch?" he asked without prelude. "We're having pizza."

"Sure, sounds great," Mac said, even though she'd had pizza last night. She would've eaten bologna sandwiches, for all she cared. She was just so eager to see Alex. "I'll put on my shoes and be right over, okay?"

"Optimal!"

Mac hung up and dashed into the bathroom, heading straight for the sink so she could brush her teeth. As she eliminated her bad breath, she stared at herself in the mirror, thinking her hair looked manic, unruly brown curls popping out all over, like she'd slept on it funny. And was that a zit on her chin?

After she spat and rinsed, she dabbed a cover-up stick on the red spot and did her best to tame her mane before slicking on vanilla Chap Stick. Then she slipped on her flip-flops and raced out of her room and down the stairs to the kitchen, where her dad and Honey were playing footsies as they read the *Houston Chronicle* in the breakfast nook, like they did every Sunday morning. Only the step-Barbie glanced up as Mac poked her head through the door.

"I'm going over to the Bishops'," she said, and Honey smiled.

"Okay, sweetie," she drawled. "Have a good time."

Her father grunted but didn't even look up from the sports page, clearly more interested in the latest Astros score than in his own daughter.

"Bye, then," Mac said quietly, trying not to feel frustrated by the way her dad avoided her. Did it hurt him too much to acknowledge she existed now and then? Did it just remind him of what he'd lost?

Stop it, Mac told herself, knowing that analyzing her father's behavior didn't do her any good. It only made her feel worse.

She flung herself out the rear French doors and onto the patio, not pausing for breath until she'd reached the tall hedge between the houses. Then she ducked through the space between the boxwoods that she and Alex had carved out when they were kids. There was even a gently worn footpath that reapplication of mulch every spring could never completely erase.

He was waiting for her on the other side, standing on the deck and pushing hair from his eyes so he could check his wristwatch.

"Hey, hey!" she shouted as she strode toward him.

Alex glanced up, and his face broke into an easy grin.

"Howdy, stranger," he said, opening up his arms as she came within range. Mac ran right into them. Her head tucked easily beneath his chin as he squeezed her for a second, and she closed her eyes, thinking how good he smelled, just as she remembered. Like Zest soap and cinnamon toast.

"You're taller, aren't you?" she asked when she pulled away, because he seemed to have grown about six inches. Mac cocked her head and looked him over, noticing all the subtle ways he'd changed, besides towering over her now.

His hair was longer, cut in choppy waves that fell in sculpted curls on his brow, just touching his collar in back. Gone were the bottle-thick glasses, replaced by small wirerims that seemed to enlarge his blue eyes rather than obscure them. He looked good, better than she remembered. Or maybe it was only the relief of having him back again.

His lopsided smile looked pleased. "Either I grew or you shrank."

Mac gave him a nudge. "Geez, what'd they feed you at computer camp, hormones?"

"Ah, *Fräulein* Mac"—he looped an arm around her shoulders and guided her inside to the Bishops' kitchen—"it was more like clean air from the Black Forest, plenty of stimulating conversation, and more beer than I could drink."

"What, no strudel?"

"Okay, maybe a little strudel too," he said, and pulled out a stool for her at the breakfast bar. As she slid atop the seat he went around to the other side, where the pizza box sat. He doled out several large slices on two plates, setting one in front of her and the other on the counter next to hers. He ripped two squares from a roll of paper towels to use as napkins, then came around and plunked down beside her.

"Well, your place looks the same as ever," Mac said, glancing around, noting as usual the startling contrast between her family's place and the Bishops'. Whereas Mac's dad insisted the house be kept spotless—which entailed Honey having domestic help—the Bishops were way more laid-back. Sure, they had granite countertops and stainless steel in their spacious kitchen like every other updated and renovated 1950s-era two-story on their street, but the room Mac surveyed was no page out of *Houston Lifestyles and Homes* magazine. The large bay windows that overlooked the backyard and pool were smudged with streaky fingerprints, and the flowers on the glass-topped breakfast table drooped over the vase. Cereal bowls littered the sink, and sections of the Sunday paper covered sections of the tiled floor.

"But it's way too quiet," she added. Despite the evidence of other human life—like the dishes in the sink and discarded newspaper—Mac didn't hear a peep. Usually Alex's nine-year-old brother, Elliott, was running around in a Superman cape with a herd of his nine-year-old comrades behind him.

"Mom and Dad took Idiot shopping for school supplies," Alex said, explaining the silence.

"Kind of last-minute, isn't it? School starts tomorrow."

"Mac, Mac, Mac"—Alex clicked tongue against teeth—"you *have* been away from this house for too long. Don't you know that the Bishops are notorious procrastinators? Didn't my parents throw a birthday party for me last year two weeks after the fact?"

Mac laughed. "I think it was more like ten years after the fact, since Chuck E. Cheese isn't exactly the hot spot for teen parties."

"Ah, but we had fun, didn't we? Almost as much fun as I had at the International Technology Symposium. Man, it was awesome," he gushed, pausing briefly to jump up and fetch Cokes from the fridge. He deposited a cold can in front of her. "So many people all in one place who spoke my language. It was like Dr. Spitznagel's AP physics class all over again."

Mac paused with a slice of pizza in hand, the gooey cheese dripping. "Oh, yeah, I remember your telling me. It was all of, what, two other Caldwell boys and you?"

He chuckled, and Mac felt something shift inside her, like a part that had been missing had settled into place again.

"Well, while you were having fun hanging with your geek homies, I had to play with Dad and Honey at Lake Conroe."

"Sounds painful." He made a face. "The real question is . . . did you *play nice*?"

Mac shrugged. "I didn't do away with her, if that's what you're asking. In fact, she was perky enough to drag me to Post Oak with her yesterday. She made me go to a day spa and then shopping."

"Good God, girl. *You* went shopping?" Alex mumbled. He looked mortified, his mouth hanging open, and it was full of food.

"Gross, dude!" Mac elbowed him. "Didn't anyone in Germany teach you how to chew with your mouth closed?"

He swallowed dutifully before he replied, "You think any of the rest of the techies I hung with had table manners? We're not debutantes, you know."

Mac dumped the pizza crust onto her plate and brushed off her hands. "Well, neither am I."

"Not yet, anyway." Alex smiled. "But you will be."

Mac's cheeks warmed. "You're assuming they'll invite me and I'll accept."

"Oh, they will, and you will," he said, sounding awfully sure of himself, or sure of her.

She squinted at him. "And you know this because . . . ?"

"I know you, Mac, and you're not a quitter."

"Being a quitter has nothing to do with it," she insisted, tensing up like she had at the sleepover when Laura had pestered her about the same thing. "Maybe it's not who I am."

"What do you want me to say? 'Be true to yourself'? 'Don't do it just because your friends are doing it'?" He had a cheeky smile on his face, like he knew something she didn't. And it bugged her immensely.

Yes, that's exactly what I want you to say!

"Precisely," she snapped, "because it's true."

"Hmm." He looked her square in the eye. "Are you sure? Or is it just what you want to hear?"

Argh! He drove her crazy when he did this, countering something they both knew was right, provoking her into questioning herself and taking a look at the other side, when all Mac wanted was for *someone* to agree with her. She sighed, tired of the whole "to debut or not to debut" argument.

She changed the subject entirely. "You have tomato sauce on your face, you know."

"I do? And I usually only get it on my shirt. Is it here?" he asked, poking at the corners of his mouth with his tongue but not quite reaching the spot.

"God, you're hopeless." Mac plucked the paper towel out of her lap and used it to wipe the red smear from his cheek. His thickly lashed blue eyes watched her from behind his wire-rims, and she felt her pulse start thumping in the oddest way.

"Okay, all clean," she said, and pulled away. "Now tell me about camp," she prodded, knowing he'd dive right in and the subject of the Rosebuds would be forgotten.

His face lit up. "Oh, man, where to start? I spent most of it building my new quad-core system, which is so much cooler than my old one, since I had to use two dual cores with a motherboard that had two processor ports, and I added RAID–" He stopped talking, no doubt sensing her bemusement. "Do you have any idea what I'm saying?"

"Nope, not a word," she replied, laughing. "But I love watching your face as you say it. You look like you did when we were eight and you took the toaster apart and put it back together."

"And my mom says that toaster was never the same."

"God, I missed you," she said, the words slipping out, and she blushed at the pleasant surprise in his face.

"I missed you too." He reached over and tousled her hair. "Same old Mac," he said. "You'll never change, will you? C'mon. Let's head upstairs to my room, shall we? My new quad-core awaits!"

Mac pushed away her empty plate. "Sure, let's go," she replied, following him toward the stairs, her enthusiasm suddenly a notch lower than it had been a mere second after he'd said "I missed you too."

Same old Mac, huh?

Mac knew she'd hardly changed at all, except maybe her hair now reached her shoulders and she'd actually tried plucking her brows after Miss Magnolia had gotten on her case about having "caterpillars" above her eyes. Maybe she should've listened to the stepbimbo about getting her bangs trimmed at the day spa.

Oh, hell, was Laura right? Had she turned into some boring reliable car?

"Do you think I'm a Honda Civic, Alex?" she asked him, hesitating with her hand on the banister.

He stopped, looking over his shoulder. "What?"

Mac shook her head. "Never mind."

She ended up hanging out with Alex all afternoon, catching up and joking around; watching *Office Space* for the umpteenth time. Until her cell rang, and it was Ginger on the other end, totally frantic.

"It's nearly five o'clock, Mac! What on earth are you doing? You need to get over here now *so we can plot how you're going to get me out of Grandmother's dinner before seven. I'll be waiting for you."*

Ginger hung up before Mac had the chance to say a single word.

"Who was that?" Alex asked as Mac stared at the phone in her hand.

"Just another friend who's lost her mind," she told him, shoving her cell back in her pocket. "I've got to run."

"Seriously?"

"Yeah, I'm sorry. I wish I could stay."

And Mac was sorry, because spending time with Alex had always been important to her. He made her feel grounded whenever she felt like the rug was being pulled out from beneath her.

"Hey, you want a ride to PFP tomorrow?" he asked as he headed down the stairs behind her. "I can pick you up at your door."

"Curbside service," she said, and took his hand in hers, squeezing it. "Sounds great. See you in the morning?"

"Cool."

Mac gave him a backhanded wave before she dashed across the wide lawn, beneath the old tree house, and around the swing set. Then she slipped through the break in the hedge, heading home as she had a million times before. Yet something felt different this time—something subtle had changed between her and Alex. It was only a feeling, nothing she could put her finger on, but it was there just the same.

It beats me how Freud could say,
"What do women want?"
as if we all want the same things.
—Katharine Whitehorn

Is there anything wrong
with being in love with something
other than money?
Or wanting a guy with soul,
even if he drives a ten-year-old Volvo?
—Ginger Fore

Eleven

Ginger sat at her grandmother's enormous mahogany dining table, linen napkin in her lap beneath her folded hands, feeling like a child again, except that her feet touched the floor and she was wearing the new blue and green V-neck sundress instead of a frilly Florence Eiseman dress with lace-trimmed socks and black patent-leather Mary Janes. She could still hear Grandmother saying, "Ah-ah-ah," in that dry Southern drawl, followed by, "Don't you remember the song I taught you, Ginger Dupree Fore? *Mabel, Mabel, if you're able, get your elbows off the table.*"

Ginger only forgot about elbows on the table when she was chowing down with Mac or Laura. Then all her lessons in manners went out the window. At least at Whataburger there weren't so many spoons and forks set out that you had to think before you picked one up.

"More tea, Miss Ginger?" asked a slim brown-skinned woman in a neat tan pantsuit, hovering beside her with an iced pitcher.

"No, thank you, Serena, I'm good."

"All right, then."

Around her, in her grandmother's River Oaks mansion,

house staff efficiently swept in and out of the room, bringing in each course on silver trays and refreshing tea and water glasses as soon as two sips were taken. There was something about being waited on hand and foot that made Ginger uneasy. Maybe it was the stiff formality of it all, or the sense of divide between master and servant, which Rose Dupree was very keen on. The house itself was equally old-fashioned, from its pillared antebellum façade to the high-ceilinged rooms overstuffed with uncomfortable antique furniture that had Ginger yearning to get back to the ultra-modern Castle.

Sometimes when she visited Rose Dupree, Ginger felt like she'd slipped back into another century, one of genteel living near downtown in a secluded enclave of tidy plots of land, stately manors, and a main boulevard with old-fashioned cast-iron streetlamps that led directly to the doors of the River Oaks Country Club. Ginger's mother had grown up in these parts and had threatened to move back after the divorce from Edward Fore was made final. But Ginger had breathed a huge sigh of relief when her father had let them have the Castle off Piney Point. Her life was centered west of the Loop, back in the Memorial Villages, while Rose Dupree's house on Piping Rock was definitely east, closer to Rice University and a zillion miles away from Ginger's world in so many ways.

God, Ginger suddenly thought, *wouldn't it have sucked if I'd ended up in River Oaks, going to St. John's and never seeing Mac or Laura?*

"Dear, are you listening to me?" her grandmother said from the head of the table, and Ginger looked up. "I was telling your mother that I wish you hadn't wasted your summer in New Orleans." Rose Dupree's slim nose wrinkled as she added, "Such a filthy place even before the hurricane, although your grandfather and I did have a lovely weekend in the French Quarter once." She waved the memory off with a wrinkled hand. "I would've been happy to speak to the Garden Club about your helping with tree planting at the wetland ecology pond near the equestrian center."

"Why, Grandmother, that's so thoughtful of you," Ginger said, and smiled what she hoped looked like a gracious smile. "Maybe next year," she offered, though she didn't really mean it.

Rose Dupree would never understand why Ginger *liked* getting her hands dirty working for Habitat in New Orleans any more than she'd ever grasp Ginger's distaste for meat of any kind—the reason Ginger had skipped the appetizer altogether, considering it was pheasant ravioli smothered in brown sauce.

Ugh.

At the moment, they were in the middle of the soup course, which was more to Ginger's liking: black bean with chopped onions, though she'd had the chef hold the sour cream.

"All right, then, I'll talk to the Garden Club next year and find a suitable summer project for you," her grandma said in her commanding drawl as she set down her soup spoon and wiped her mouth daintily with a lace-edged napkin. "At least I won't have to worry about you consorting with inappropriate girls when you're a Glass Slipper debutante," Rose Dupree went on, frowning as she turned to look at Ginger's mother. "Remember, Deena, when the selection committee unwisely elected that liberal woman to chair and she nearly

149

allowed a colored girl in? Thank heavens Bootsie Bidwell's in charge, so Ginger won't have to deal with anything like that in her class of debs."

Colored girl?

Dear God.

Ginger choked on a spoonful of black bean soup, quickly drawing her napkin to her mouth while Deena Fore exclaimed, "For heaven's sake, Mother, Amanda Cleverly was hardly a liberal!"

"She was a Democrat, wasn't she?" Rose said accusingly, waving a hand in the air. "Same difference."

Ginger's mom rolled her eyes and let the subject drop, obviously used to hearing her mother's archaic comments and clearly aware that arguing with Rose Dupree was an exercise in futility. The older woman was set in her ways, and nothing anyone could say or do would change that. Ginger had tried on more than one occasion until she was red in the face.

As if nothing disagreeable had been discussed a mere minute before, Rose shifted her attention to Ginger, her age-worn face softening. "So, my angel, your momma tells me you'd like to wear my gown for your debut. Is that so?"

Ginger glanced across the table at her mother and saw Deena's slender shoulders stiffen beneath her silk Chanel blouse. That alone told Ginger plenty. Deena was all too good at hiding how she really felt behind a pasted-on smile. Her perfectly made-up features betrayed nothing, though Ginger noticed how she kept reaching up to tuck her short blond hair behind her ear.

"Well?" her grandmother pressed, peering down at Ginger from the head of the long table as Deena watched her daughter, waiting to hear what she had to say.

Ginger set her spoon on the small plate beneath her soup bowl, cleared her throat, and replied, "I would kill to wear your gown, Grandmother, if that's okay. Mom's a little worried I might mess it up or something."

"Is that true, Deena?"

Rose Dupree shifted her gaze from Ginger to Deena without moving her head. Even at seventy, Ginger's grandmother looked stylish in the way of proper Southern ladies, with her white hair neatly bobbed, a double strand of cultured pearls at her throat, and slashes of pink lipstick across her broad mouth. Rose Dupree always said a well-bred woman never went anywhere without her pearls and her lipstick.

"Well, I hadn't given Ginger any real answer, Mother, not yet," Deena Fore confessed, and set down her soup spoon to snatch up her gin and tonic. Ginger had already seen the drink replaced several times. "I'm merely worried she'll spill something on it or tear it, or otherwise ruin it forever."

"My dear, what's the point of savin' the thing if my own granddaughter can't use it? You figurin' on having it preserved in a museum?" Silver eyebrows arched over hazel eyes, and Deena backed down.

"Well, no, I . . . of course, I wasn't," her mother replied, practically stuttering. "But I had expected you might want to donate it to the Glass Slipper Club's archives one day."

"Then we'll do it after Ginger's debut." Rose Dupree waved a wrinkled and beringed hand dismissively. "I think it's a grand idea, sweet child," she said, and bestowed a smile upon Ginger, the kind that Ginger noticed Deena rarely received.

"Thank you, Grammy." Ginger used the pet name she'd used as a little girl, and Rose beamed.

"Then that's that"—Rose clapped silently—"so now we'll just have to decide who your peer escort should be, and if we should allow that heathen of a father of yours to participate after he walked out on your mother to marry that trollop."

"Mother, please!" Deena choked on her cocktail.

Rose ignored her. "And, of course, we'll have to get you a new wardrobe for all the luncheons and teas, and we'll have to talk about your choice of philanthropy."

Ginger chewed on the inside of her cheek rather than responding, because she knew by now it would do no good. Her grandmother had a way of mowing over everyone and everything, if she had a mind to; the only way Ginger could get what she wanted was to subversively do it herself.

So she let Rose and Deena argue back and forth about escorts and wardrobe and charities while she nervously fingered her Razr phone, set on vibrate and stuck in the pocket of her sundress. Mac was supposed to call any minute to get her out of there so she could run home, change, stuff her knapsack with Luna Bars, and fill a Nalgene bottle with water before she met Javier. Thank God her mother had driven to Rose's straight from a house showing so that Ginger had her own car. Otherwise, she would've had to make Mac zip over to River Oaks and retrieve her.

C'mon, girlfriend, she thought, *do your thing!*

But the soup bowls were being cleared and the salad was being served already, and the clock on the mantel chimed softly once, indicating it was a half hour past six.

What is holding Mac up?

Another agonizing five minutes ticked by before she felt the phone vibrate against her thigh. She knew her grandmother would think her an ill-mannered boor for answering her cell at the table, but she didn't care.

She flipped it open and whipped it up to her ear, making horrible faces as she said a bunch of "ohmigawd's" and "oh, no's," though Mac had hung up already. Ginger scooted back her chair and stood, her napkin falling from her lap.

"For heaven's sake, Ginger," Deena said, looking horrified, "put that thing away and sit down."

"But it's Mac," she shot back, making herself sound as upset as possible. Then she went to her grandmother's side and kneeled beside her chair. "You know Mac Mackenzie, Grandmother, she's been one of my very best friends since kindergarten, and she's in trouble." Ginger began spewing out the lie she'd made up earlier. "Mac's car broke down on the freeway, and her parents aren't answering their phones and she can't find Laura anywhere. She's got a tow truck coming, but it's taking her car somewhere downtown, and she's all freaked out." Ginger paused for breath.

Rose Dupree's forehead wrinkled with concern. "My goodness, child, we'll have my driver go fetch her. It's no problem."

"No!" Ginger yelped, not having seen that one coming. "She specifically asked if I'd come get her, Grammy, and I promised I'd go. I can't leave her there waiting for your driver. She's crying and everything."

"Dear Lord," Deena murmured. "You'd think she could call a cab."

Deena's eye-rolling response was apparently all the motivation Rose needed to instruct Ginger, "Go, sweet girl. Go on and help your poor friend. Your momma and I will finish dinner, and maybe you can bring Miss Mackenzie back here for dessert, if all goes well."

"Thanks, Grammy! I knew you'd understand," Ginger said, breathing a huge sigh of relief. She snatched her purse and took off before Rose Dupree could change her mind.

* * *

"So you're going to be a debutante? I'm no rich boy, so I don't know all the crazy things you blue bloods do. Is it anything like my sister's *quinceañera*?" Javier asked beside her.

They were each handcuffed to the heavy chain he'd wrapped around the two-hundred-year-old oak tree in the private park adjacent to Ginger's school, which meant they could do little but sit side by side, their backs against the bark, swatting at mosquitoes with their free hands and watching the sweat stains on their clothes expand.

So much for Ginger's goal of impressing Javier as a serious environmentalist, since the first thing he'd done after she'd shown up was to critique her outfit–"Why're you wearing shorts, *chiquita*? And sandals? You want the bugs to eat you alive?"–and loan her his bottle of Skin-So-Soft.

Two hours had passed since then, according to the clock on Ginger's Razr, and nothing even remotely exciting had happened. No one had even seemed to glance twice at them, save for a few joggers brave enough to withstand the heat, and even they had only quickly looked over, panting as they staggered past, the perspiration dripping down their faces probably blinding them. Or else the sight of a man and woman chained to a tree just wasn't the shock it should've been.

The sun had begun to set, and the sky was finally less a blazing blue and more a cotton-candy pink. If they were lucky, it might start to cool down into the eighties. At nine o'clock, it still felt closer to triple digits.

Ginger had already downed half the water from the Nalgene bottle and was starting to feel the need to pee, which might be a tad complicated, all things considered.

"Did you hear what I said?" Javier nudged her.

"*Quinceañera,*" Ginger repeated, feeling stupid, because she didn't even know what that was. "Is that like a birthday party?" she guessed.

"Yeah, it's sort of a birthday party," he said, and smiled at her. "It means fifteen years, but it's more like a sweet sixteen party over here."

"Over here? Like west of the Loop?"

"No. I mean, the U.S.," he laughed. "I wasn't born in Texas, you know. We came from Mexico City when I was a kid. Does that bother you, *chica estropeada,* hanging out with a dude like me?"

"What's *estrop* . . . whatever you said?" she asked, since the term wasn't in her limited vocabulary of Spanish (though she had a pretty good idea that it wasn't complimentary).

"*Estropeada,*" Javier repeated, and grinned even wider. "It means 'spoiled,' " he said. "Because that's what you are. You live in a big fancy house with a big fancy yard, and your father's name is in the newspaper every other day. You're like the H-town Paris Hilton."

"Gee, thanks."

She got a little tired of him tossing words like "blue blood," "princess," or "spoiled" into every conversation.

155

Now he'd just majorly dissed her by comparing her to the biggest piece of debu-trash on the planet?

"Okay, so you're not like Paris. You damn sure don't dress as hot. I don't figure they make miniskirts and peeka-boo lingerie in hemp, do they?"

She opened her mouth to say something back, but ended up biting her lip and saying nothing.

Well, hell. Not only is he basically stating outright that I'm not hot, but he's patronizing me because my family has money. Like it's my fault I'm spoiled.

"Aw, don't get upset." He took her free hand in his and squeezed it. "I'm just teasing, *amiga*. Paris Hilton's such a *puta*. You're much better than she is, even if you are as stink-ing rich."

"Stop it," she snapped, jerking her hand away and sticking it between her sweaty knees.

She suddenly felt dirty and disappointed that this wasn't going anywhere near as well as she'd imagined. No camera crews had shown up, no one even seemed to care that they were there, none of Javier's ecoconscious friends had joined them, and Javier had pretty much treated her like a little sister since she'd arrived, mostly bossing her around, instructing her on where to sit and how to cuff her wrist so her arm wouldn't go numb, and eating all four granola bars she'd brought.

Now he'd insulted her, and she was hot and pissed off and beginning to question her judgment about showing up at all. Staying at her grandmother's and watching Rose and Deena go at it would've been more fun than this.

"If I'm such a spoiled brat, why am I here, huh? 'Cuz I don't see anyone else sitting with you, chained to a damned tree in ninety-five-degree heat." Tears sprang to her eyes.

"Why don't you just take the key and unlock my cuffs so I can go home to my big fancy house?"

"Ah, but you're the only one I wanted with me tonight, *debutante*," he assured her, but he said it "day-boo-tan-tey," which sounded almost romantic, especially the way his voice purred.

Ginger sighed, her insides threatening to turn to mush. Javier knew just how to twist her snugly around his little finger when he wanted to.

"Please, stay? I need you here." He grabbed her hand again and held it more firmly this time, so she couldn't easily slide her fingers from his.

For a moment, she didn't respond. She sat there and stared in the other direction, squinting at the yellow earthmover equipment silently waiting about five yards away. It reminded her why she was here—why she was *supposed* to be here—and it had nothing to do with convincing Javier she was dateworthy (although that had certainly weighed heavily on her decision to come in the first place).

Mac and Laura had both accused her of being half-assed about her passion for green causes, and this was a chance to prove them wrong. Even if it meant being chained to a guy she'd thought she cared about who was acting like a total dick.

"I'll stay," she finally said, still not looking at him.

He breathed an audible sigh of relief.

"But it has nothing to do with your apology," she added, only half-lying. "I'm here for the tree."

"Of course you are, *chica*," he cooed. "You're very special. You care about important things, not just the labels in your jeans."

So she was special, huh? Okay, so she wasn't hating him quite so much anymore. He was probably just stressed out, worried that the Sam Houston Oak would be bulldozed in the morning, despite anything they did.

"I like you, Ginger," Javier said, surprising her with the admission. "Don't you like being here with me?"

She shrugged. "A little."

"Well, that's a start." He squeezed her hand again. "Hey, don't worry so much about nothing happening yet. I've got friends working on things, making calls and sending e-mails and text messages. There'll be action, very soon. You trust me, don't you?"

She nodded, feeling the electricity from his touch coursing through her. If he couldn't sense the chemistry too, then he was completely oblivious.

Javier nudged her with his shoulder. "Now tell me about this debut of yours. My sister's party was at the parish hall at St. Cecilia's, after a special Mass. I'll bet your party's nothing like that, huh?"

Ginger loved the way his eyes crinkled and how white his teeth seemed against his dark skin. She leaned her head against the bark. "It's kind of like a rite of passage, I guess," she explained. "But it's more of an introduction to society."

"Ah, so the rich boys notice you," he said.

"It's a tradition, like if your mother debuted, then you're supposed to follow suit. Besides, what makes you think I like rich boys?" She watched his dark eyebrows arch. "Maybe I'm doing it because I figure I can use my position for something important."

Javier actually looked interested. "So what do you have to do before you can go through this rite of passage?"

"They make you take classes in etiquette and ballroom dancing, even if you've done it before, and they teach you how to write thank-you notes and how to use all the spoons and forks in a place setting, though my grandmother drilled that into my head since the time I was old enough to sit up straight."

"Anything else?"

Ginger didn't know how much he wanted to hear. "There are teas and luncheons and all kinds of functions so the debs get to know each other, and get to know the guys who'll be everyone's escorts, although it's our fathers who present us, sort of like giving us away at a wedding."

"I see." Javier shifted positions, turning slightly toward her, resting his free arm on his knee; the other remained awkwardly cuffed to the chain around the tree. "So who gets to choose your date for you? Your parents?"

"God, I hope not. Not my grandmother, either." Ginger laughed, glancing over and meeting his gaze, holding it long enough to make her blush.

Was that a hint, perhaps? Did he want to go with her? *Ohmigawd!* Wouldn't her mother and Rose Dupree just *die* if she took him?

Before she could even suggest it in jest, he asked, "So what do you wear to your debutante ball? Something expensive and beautiful, I bet."

Ginger wet her lips; the moment between them passed. "Each Rosebud has to wear something white, like a bridal gown. And no one can wear the same thing, so there's even a party where all the girls bring their dresses and register them. One of the Glass Slipper Club ladies keeps a list and photographs to make sure they're all different."

Javier shook his head. "You're shitting me, right?"

"No."

"And you would do all this because . . . ?"

She picked at the grass that tickled her feet. "I think traditions are important," she said, "but it's more than that. I'm trying to carve a place for myself and have a voice so that I can stand up for something."

"Honoring what's come before you can be a good thing," Javier said softly. "If it's something you really believe in." He tucked his thumb beneath her chin and made her look right at him, into his eyes. "It's a rite of passage in itself to put yourself on the line and risk everything, even your family. Maybe you should tell your father to go to hell, because what he's doing is the wrong thing. *That* would be standing up for something."

What the heck was that about? she wondered. What did Edward Fore have to do with anything?

She was glad dusk was rapidly descending, as she hated the way he seemed to be searching her face for something that wasn't there, maybe looking for a depth he didn't think she had. She felt on the verge of telling him more about herself than most people knew: why she was always searching for a cause to believe in and how she'd nearly been cut in two by her father deserting her and her mother seeking solace in booze.

But she didn't get the chance.

With a crackle of tires on gravel and the rattle of engines, a trio of media vans appeared, veering off onto the grass. Headlights flooded the descending darkness, causing Ginger to squint into the glare, blinded like a deer in headlights.

"Ah, perfect timing. Here we go," Javier said, letting her

go. "*Lo siento*. . . . I'm sorry if I hurt you, *chica,* but I didn't have a choice."

Hurt me?

Ginger wanted to ask what he meant, but Javier was already focused on the descending swarm of media.

He struggled to his feet one-handed, not offering to help her up.

So Ginger stayed on the ground, bracing her back against the tree as the reporters and their cameramen raced toward them, microphones at the ready, clearly anxious to get something for the ten o'clock news.

Before a single question had even been flung at him, Javier went off, like a verbal time bomb.

"They want to tear down this two-hundred-year-old piece of history to make room for a bigger parking lot for a school that caters to the most privileged girls in the city," he spat out as the cameras rolled, "when this Sam Houston Oak has been here longer than all of us. Houston himself reportedly took shade here and carved his initials in the trunk, but does anyone care? It's a travesty, a disgusting show of greed, tearing up a vital link to our Texas heritage to pave the ground with more asphalt."

His voice was strong, impassioned, and devoid of the accent she heard when they conversed and he called her *"amiga"* or *"chica."* He sounded like an Anglo, although he looked like anything but: dark eyes flashing fire, sooty hair slick against his face, one hand wildly gesticulating.

"What's your name?" a reporter asked him, though Ginger couldn't even see who it was with the lights from the cameras in her eyes.

"My name isn't important," he replied, and abruptly

turned to Ginger, pointing down at her. "But hers is. This girl beside me, defending the oak as I am, she's someone whose name should be very familiar. She's the daughter of Edward Fore of E. W. Fore Development, the company handing over this land to Pine Forest Prep, where his daughter goes . . . his privileged little debutante."

Even if she hadn't been shackled to the oak, Ginger couldn't have moved; she could barely breathe.

My father's company owns the land? They're *the ones who are going to cut down the tree?*

And Javier had known it all along?

Ohmifreakinggawd.

No wonder she was the only one he'd needed by his side this evening. It had nothing to do with respecting her as a comrade-in-arms or even wanting to spend time with her. He'd involved her in this particular mission so he could use her name, pit her against her father, and then throw her to the wolves.

She felt sick to her stomach. She closed her eyes as Javier went on and on, her mind spinning dizzily. She wished this could all be over and she could go home.

Does Laura feel like this every time Avery shows up wanting a piece of her, but not her heart? Does she feel betrayed and used?

Because that was exactly how Ginger felt. She hadn't even slept with Javier, and he'd still managed to screw her over but good.

"Stop it," she got out, but Javier either couldn't hear her or wasn't listening.

Besides, it was already too late.

She heard the sirens approach well before the swirls of blue and red filled the night. Car doors slammed and voices ordered, "Move aside, please." Then the cops were right there in front of them. Javier told them, "Do you know who she is? She's Ginger Fore. Her father owns the development company that's razing the tree and turning over the land to the school. *Her* school! She's here to protest the total disregard that her father and her exclusive prep school are showing for the planet."

But the police didn't seem to care whose daughter she was, not the way the reporters did.

While Javier continued to rant, the boys in blue used bolt cutters to free them and led them separately to waiting squad cars, the media filming every minute and Javier shouting, "*¡Viva el árbol!* Let the tree live!"

A strong hand settled on Ginger's head, pushing it down and guiding her into the backseat, closing the door firmly behind her, the vehicle rocking underneath. It smelled of vinyl and deodorizer and vaguely of pee, but Ginger sat dazed, too numb to do anything but stare out the window quietly, watching the familiar landscape passing by beneath the streetlights.

It wasn't long until they'd reached the Memorial Villages police station and she was marched inside and taken to a small room with a table and chairs. She wasn't fingerprinted, though she dared to ask in a voice bordering on hysterical, "Am I under arrest?"

"Not yet, young lady, you're just being detained," said the policewoman who was apparently in charge of her. "I believe the chief called your father, and he's on his way down."

Her father was coming down to the police station to get her? Like she wasn't embarrassed enough.

Oh, God, what have I done?

Ginger wasn't sure she could face him.

It was both the longest and shortest ten minutes of her life before Edward Fore showed up, looking more worried than angry: his mouth tightly pursed, his pale eyes frantic, his faded red hair combed neatly over his freckled scalp. He was wearing a tux with onyx cuff links and polished Bruno Magli shoes, which meant he'd been torn away from a black-tie function. If he'd opened his mouth and ripped her head off, Ginger wouldn't have been a bit surprised. Her mother would've started in on her the moment she'd walked through the door.

Instead, he opened his arms as he came toward her, asking only, "Are you all right, baby girl?"

"Daddy, I'm sorry," Ginger said, and then she burst into tears.

Always be nice to other girls.
If you don't, they will find
some underhanded way
of getting even with you.
—Elizabeth Hawes

I can't imagine anything lamer
than being called *nice*.
—Jo Lynn Bidwell

Twelve

Jo Lynn didn't drag herself out of bed until late on Sunday afternoon. Once she threw off the tangled sheets, she was tempted to crawl back in again after catching her reflection in the full-length mirror. Talk about a hot mess. She squinted through puffy eyes ringed by raccoonlike smudges of dark mascara and tried to drag her fingers through her knotty hair. It was a good thing Dillon couldn't see her now. Mixing the Xanax with margaritas wasn't such a great idea, and neither was staying up until five a.m., doing her best to forget her disrupted seduction of Dillon. She had a banging hangover as a souvenir.

It was four p.m. when she emerged from the guesthouse's master bedroom and shuffled into the galley kitchen, desperate for a cup of coffee. She completely ignored the detritus from the party, which filled the sink and covered the countertops as well as littering the living room. That was the housekeeper's job, not hers.

When the coffee finally brewed, she swallowed two Excedrin with the first cup. She downed a second cup before she felt anything close to civilized. Sobered up, she checked her cell for messages, and there were plenty of them, mostly from Cam and Trisha, one from Danielle Bartlett, another from Kelly Harms.

But nothing from Dillon, not even a text. What was up with that?

She speed-dialed his number and let it ring until she heard his voice saying, "Hey, it's Dillon. Whassup?"

Jo perked up. "Dill, it's me," she rushed to say, and then realized she was talking to his voice mail when she heard the ensuing beep.

She hung on a few seconds, finally blurting, "Hey, it's Jo. Call me," before she slapped her cell closed. What other message could she possibly leave? Something pathetic along the lines of *Where are you? Why'd you leave me last night? Was that phone call really an emergency, or were you with someone else?*

No, no, no.

Stop it, Jo, she told herself.

Playing guessing games only made it worse. She'd let Dill come to her if he had something to say. She wouldn't nag him to death, since that never worked and was the surest way to drive a guy off forever.

That settled in her head, Jo Lynn showered and changed into a pair of Abercrombie shorts and a T-shirt, then left the guesthouse, taking her time walking back to the main house.

For a while, she sat on the pool's edge with her legs dangling in the water, but she quickly found herself thinking of Dillon again and wondering what was wrong with him . . . or wrong with her. Why couldn't they seem to get together anymore? He'd said that he loved her, right? So what was really going on? It was almost as though he was avoiding her, or at least avoiding *sex* with her.

God, it was all so depressing.

She got up and brushed the water from her legs, which was when she spotted the satin Christian Louboutin high heels lying on the tiles and backflashed on her run-in with Laura Bell the night before.

Has Big Dill stopped jonesing for you too, like every other guy does when he realizes you're as hollow inside as a cheap chocolate Easter bunny?

Laura's taunt ran through her head again and again, and Jo Lynn felt a burst of raw anger pulse through her. That poseur had dissed *her*?

Puh-leeze.

Laura was a fool for believing the in crowd would ever accept her, not at her size.

Talk about naïve. Jo Lynn had only been nice to her as a lark when Avery had first started bringing her around, because it had seemed like a really bad joke, like he was using the besotted Laura to prove that he could do whatever—and *whomever*—he wanted. Unfortunately, when Bootsie had learned that Laura was dating Avery, she'd gotten all excited. Just because Jo Lynn's mother and Tincy Bell were such great pals, Bootsie figured it could be the same for their daughters. Like Jo Lynn and Laura becoming BFF was ever going to happen. Not even if pigs—or Laura—could fly.

At least Avery had come to his senses back then, chucking Laura for more suitable girls—like Camie, for one—until he'd dipped his toes back into the swamp waters. Sometimes guys were so damned slow.

Jo Lynn grabbed the Louboutins and tossed them into the pool. Then she stood and watched each one sink to the bottom, feeling vindicated as they settled near the drain.

Down the drain was exactly where Laura would be headed

once Jo Lynn had her way. Camie and Trish were right. They had to do something to keep that debu-tank from getting on the Rosebud list. Imagining the lard-ass in white gloves and gown just didn't sit right.

That decided, Jo Lynn marched toward the main house, letting herself into the kitchen. Nan was there, looking a little hungover herself, no surprise after the bottle of merlot she'd put down. She was yakking with Cookie about something, though they stopped talking the minute Jo Lynn entered.

"Could you have someone clean up the guest house," Jo said, an order, not a question. She pulled open the fridge and grabbed a tub of yogurt. "It's a little messy after my friends came by last night."

"Yes, miss, of course," Nan said, none too brightly.

"By any chance, did Dillon call on the landline?" Jo Lynn reluctantly asked, and she could swear Nan's face got all smug when she answered.

"No, miss, no one's called for you on the house telephone."

"Oh, all right." Jo Lynn grabbed a spoon and headed off.

"Um, miss," Nan called after her, "your mother's home and she'd like to see you upstairs."

Jo Lynn stopped in her tracks. *Great,* she thought, suddenly losing her appetite. She left the yogurt and the spoon on the counter, squared her shoulders, and trudged from the kitchen, through the foyer, and up the winding stairwell.

Jo Lynn knocked on the half-opened door to the master suite, waiting for her mother's coolly delivered "Yes, come in" before she entered.

Bootsie was unpacking and had clothes spread out across

the king-sized sleigh bed. Jo's father was nowhere in sight. Probably on the golf course, she figured, or at the office, catching up on whatever he'd missed. He was such a workaholic.

"Ah, it's you, baby," Bootsie said, and put down the blouse she'd been holding. She opened her arms, wiggling manicured fingers. "Come give your mother a kiss."

Jo Lynn crossed the room and stepped into her mother's light embrace, Bootsie's hands barely grazing her arms. Her mother's lips just brushed each of her cheeks before she drew away.

"You look tired." Her mother reached out to fuss with her hair, tucking loose strands behind Jo Lynn's ears. "I guess you didn't get your beauty sleep, did you? Should I call the spa and have them fit you in? Your pores are looking large, sweetheart, and your hair has a funny tinge."

"I went swimming last night," Jo Lynn said, pulling away, not in the mood for Bootsie's criticism.

"I hope you stayed in the shallow end," her mother remarked, adding, "How was your party? Nan said you had some friends over."

So much for the expensive wine making Nanny Nan keep her big mouth shut, Jo Lynn thought. *Next time, I'll give her a crappy bottle of Arbor Mist.*

She shrugged. "It was nothing, really, just a few peeps getting together before school starts. But someone uninvited showed up too," she mentioned, and felt her pulse quicken.

"Oh?" Bootsie arched a carefully plucked brow. "Who?"

"Laura Bell," Jo Lynn tossed out, just to see how her mother reacted.

"Didn't you girls have a tiff last year? Over a boy, if I remember correctly." Bootsie stood stock-still for a moment, contemplating. She had not a hair out of place, as always, and her St. John summer suit was perfectly pressed, despite the brief flight on Daddy's jet. "Does that mean y'all have patched things up?"

"Hardly," Jo Lynn said, and decided to nix any attempt at suggesting to Bootsie that Laura be dropped from the Rosebud list. It would take too much explaining. How could she even *begin* to make her mom understand that every time she saw Laura Bell it was like looking into a fun-house mirror, seeing everything she never wanted to be? Everything her pageant days had taught her to despise. And the fact that Laura didn't seem to *care* how she looked made Jo insane. The cow didn't even *want* to change. Her mother had packed her off to fat camp, and she obviously hadn't lost an ounce of beef. *What a worthless waste of space.*

"So you and Laura still aren't getting along?" Bootsie pried.

Jo Lynn avoided her mother's eyes and murmured, "We're just not into the same things, Mother, and she has different friends."

"Oh, but that could change." Bootsie clicked her tongue against her teeth and smiled, her Chanel Coco Red lips curving, though the skin on her face didn't so much as crease.

"I've got a feelin' that you and Laura will reconnect once you're both Rosebuds. And it won't be long, will it?"

"Does that mean the committee has the list made up?"

"The calligrapher's on standby as we speak, waiting for the final names. It won't be much longer, peaches. Just a few days. So hold tight," Bootsie advised. "Now, if you'll excuse me, I need to get these things put away, and the rest Nan can take to the cleaners."

"Sure," Jo Lynn said, giving her mom a forced smile before she left the room. She paused in the hallway, worrying about the invitations, knowing they'd go out via private messenger in the next forty-eight hours. If she, Cam, and Trish were going to devise a plan to stop Laura from becoming a Rosebud, there wasn't much time to do it.

As soon as she was well out of Bootsie's earshot, she dialed her BFFs and arranged an ASAP confab at the Starbucks on Memorial Drive.

* * *

Jo Lynn had their favorite table on the far side of Starbucks and a grande nonfat Caffé Latte in hand when Camie and Trish appeared, both wearing Daisy Dukes, tight tank tops with their bra straps hanging out, and platform wedges. They spotted her and gave a wave before they got in line to order, and Jo Lynn glimpsed their backsides and the whale tails of their lacy thongs peeking out above the tiny denim shorts.

Was it Dress Like Twins Day and no one had told her? she mused, feeling snarky.

When Camie and Trisha each had a steaming cup of coffee in hand and chocolate biscotti to nibble on, Jo Lynn decided it was time to start plotting Laura Bell's downfall.

"I've got an idea," she started out, keeping her voice low, "of how we can blow any chance of that skank becoming a Rosebud. But we have to move fast."

"Ooo, do tell," Camie said, and Trisha leaned in.

"Remember those photos we took? Why don't we print out an anonymous note with the nastiest of those and arrange for a few special deliveries to the GSC selection committee," Jo Lynn laid out. "And just to drive the dagger in deeper, I've got a little something extra that you can do, Miss Camie, and it involves Avery."

"You know I'm in, girlfriend." Camie nodded.

"Me too," Trisha replied.

"Okay then." Jo Lynn smiled. "This is how we do it."

An hour later, the plot in place, they got up and left their table littered with empty cups, used napkins, and biscotti crumbs. Jo waved goodbye to her buds in the parking lot and slid behind the wheel of her Audi A8, the Valcona leather sighing softly beneath her as she settled in. She used the voice control to turn the radio up so the Fray filled her ears. She'd barely pulled out of the parking lot when her iPhone squealed with a text message from Dillon: Sorry abt last nite. Will make it up 2 U.

Jo Lynn was so psyched at hearing from him she could hardly keep her car in the lane. She texted back: U better! ILY BTW.

Dillon's response: ILY2.

Jo was grinning madly by the time she sailed the Audi into her driveway, parking directly behind her mother's white Escalade. Not only was she beyond psyched that Dillon had apologized, but she could hardly wait until Bootsie and her committee got her little surprise tomorrow. Wouldn't they all be shocked as hell when an ape-sized monkey wrench got tossed into the deb selection process and they had to go back to the drawing board?

Jo Lynn sighed happily as she let herself into the house and jogged up the stairs to her oversized bedroom suite. She tossed her bag onto a chair and flopped onto her bed, hitting the remote that raised the flat-screen TV from the foot-board. She was in the mood to chill in her final hours of freedom, before her senior year at PFP started with the shriek of her alarm waking her up at the crack of dawn. As she surfed through the local stations, she glimpsed a plug for the ten o'clock news and stopped right where she was, sitting up straighter.

"And on the local front, a teenager from a prominent Houston family was detained by police after protesting the destruction of the two-hundred-year-old oak known as the Sam Houston Oak. The catch? Her father's the one who donated the property to Pine Forest Preparatory Academy. More on that story at ten."

"No way," she murmured, watching a brief video clip of a redheaded girl being deposited in the backseat of a Villages police car.

Was that Green Girl, Ginger Fore?

It had sure looked like her, only with shorter hair than Jo remembered.

A teenager from a prominent Houston family whose father donated property to Pine Forest Preparatory Academy?

Yep, it had to be.

Instantly, her cell began ringing, and Jo snatched it up.

"Did you see what I saw?" It was Camie.

"Oh, yeah, and if I didn't know better, I'd think it was Christmas."

"You think the GSC will boot Miss Ginger off the list, even if her grandmother debuted at the first Rosebud Ball, like yours?" Camie sounded more excited than when she'd gotten liposuction on her butt for her birthday.

"Even great-granddaughters of Glass Slipper Club

founders won't get cut any slack if they've got a rap sheet," Jo Lynn assured her, thinking all the while that tomorrow would be a day that would live in infamy, once Laura Bell got her big ass kicked.

Jo Lynn couldn't think of any better way to start her senior year.

I think the measure of your success,
to a certain extent, will be the amount
of things written about you that aren't true.
—Cybill Shepherd

I love to gossip about other people.
I just don't like thinking other people
love to gossip about *me*.
—Laura Bell

Thirteen

Laura couldn't get down more than a piece of toast and glass of juice before she left the house extra-early on Monday morning. She usually devoured a spinach-and-feta omelet but couldn't stomach one when she was all butterflies. She had a million things to worry about besides first-day jitters, like when the Rosebud invitations would go out and whether she'd get one, whether she'd bump into Jo Lynn Bitchwell at PFP when she was without Mac or Ginger to protect her, and why Avery hadn't called her since he'd carried her to her car after her catfight with Jo Lynn on Saturday night.

At least she wouldn't be arriving at school by herself. Ginger had called late the night before, begging for a ride because the keys to her Prius had been confiscated by her pissed-off mother. She'd also been grounded for a month after getting hauled into the police station for handcuffing herself to a tree with some ecoterrorist-in-training named Javier. Apparently, Ginger had been keeping secrets lately too.

Who exactly is this Javier dude, and when did he come into the picture? Laura wondered as she wove through traffic, finally reaching Fore's Way off Piney Point and making a hard right. *Is he someone Ginger hooked up with in Louisiana?*

Laura had a few questions ready when she pulled up her Mercedes Roadster in front of the Castle. Before she'd even honked the horn, Ginger was out the door and hurrying toward the car. Laura wiggled her fingers when she spotted Deena Fore standing in the doorway, monitoring Ginger's progress to the car.

"Come straight home after school," Laura heard Mrs. Fore yell after her as Ginger opened the door and climbed inside.

"God, I feel like I'm on parole," Ginger muttered as she worked on her seat belt.

Her spiky red hair had been tamed into flatter layers, making her do nearly as conservative as their school uniform of white button-down shirt with knee-length black and tan plaid skirt. Only Ginger's stack-heeled Mary Janes belied her prissy schoolgirl image.

"You okay?" Laura asked as her friend wedged her knapsack between her legs. "Your parents came down on you hard, huh?"

Ginger's eyes looked tired and a little puffy, like she'd done her share of crying. "Obviously, my mother freaked." She glanced out the window toward where Deena Fore had been standing not a minute ago. "My dad wasn't happy either, not when he had to come down to pick me up from the police station in the middle of some big dinner party. He was wearing a tux."

"Did you get the lecture?"

"The 'I'm so disappointed in you' shtick?"

"That's the one," Laura said as she headed out of Fore Way back onto Piney Point.

Ginger held up two fingers. "I heard it twice, from him

180

and my mom, who got on the phone immediately to my grandmother. Then good ol' Rose called Bootsie Bidwell to assure her I didn't have a police record or anything and that this tiny indiscretion shouldn't affect my becoming a Rosebud."

"Holy shiz" slipped out of Laura's mouth, because getting dropped from the deb list surely sounded more horrifying to her than getting fingerprinted by the Memorial Villages Police Department.

"So now Deena's keeping me prisoner for the next month, until I 'come to my senses,' as she puts it. Although, of course, I'm allowed out for Rosebud functions"—Ginger snorted—"if I don't get myself booted."

"You won't," Laura tried to reassure her, dropping one hand from the steering wheel to squeeze her friend's arm. "Your dad's too big in this town, and your grandmother was in the first class of Rosebuds. It would take a lot more than doing something crazy for the committee to cut you down."

"I hope you're right." Ginger nibbled on her bottom lip. "My dad's donating a boatload of money to PFP to 'calm the waters,' as he put it. Enough so they can build that new library they've been raising funds for."

"Leave it to the great Edward Fore to smooth things over," Laura said. "Your dad's a pro. My father would probably just offer the school new toilet seats for the bathrooms."

If she expected Ginger to laugh, she was off the mark.

"I guess we'll know if I'm dead or alive soon enough, huh?" Ginger remarked, her voice as low-key as the rest of her. She turned her head then to glance out the window, and suddenly there was silence.

Laura decided maybe it was best just to leave her alone, though she hated the quiet because it gave her time to dwell on her own troubles. Would Jo Lynn seek revenge because Laura had crashed her party? More importantly, what was with Avery's disappearing act? She hadn't gotten so much as a text from him, and she'd been fighting the urge to make first contact. What had happened when he'd gone back to "smooth things over" with the Bimbo Cartel after he'd deposited Laura at her Merc? Had Jo Lynn brainwashed him again and convinced him to stay away from Laura because she wasn't worthy? Or was it something much, much worse?

God forbid he'd gotten back together with Camie Lindell. If he had, Laura wasn't sure she could ever look him in the eye again, not after the way she'd opened up to him when they'd gone back to her house from the airport.

Stop inventing bad things before they've happened, she told herself, and relaxed her tight grip on the steering wheel. Somewhat calmer, she guided her Roadster down Taylorcrest toward the intersection with Strey Lane, where Pine Forest Prep sat on a huge corner lot bordered by towering pine trees. She turned the radio on and then off again when she could find nothing but morning talk-jocks yammering.

Within a quarter mile of the school, they hit a major traffic jam, vehicles bumper to bumper. The first day of school was always like this, with all the overprotective parents wanting to drop off their own children rather than carpool. It made one hell of a mess. But it gave Laura a chance to ask Ginger the question she'd been dying to ask.

"So," she started in gently, "what about this Javier Garcia?

I saw his picture in this morning's paper. He looks hot, girl-friend. How come you never mentioned him before?"

Ginger looked over and gave in to a sly smile. "He's too hot for his own good, and he's smart and passionate. . . ."

"Ooooh."

"About the *environment*," Ginger clarified, rightly assuming Laura had jumped to her own conclusions. "*And* he's a really gifted painter. He was doing a mural on our dining room wall until Deena fired him this morning." She stopped smiling, and her expression tightened. "I thought he was one of those pathologically honest people, you know? But he's a stone-cold liar. I mean, he used me because I'm Edward Fore's daughter."

"Maybe he didn't mean to."

"How could he not mean to?" Ginger scoffed. "He obviously had everything planned all along. He knew that I was his key to getting media coverage, and he didn't care how I'd feel when I realized what was up."

"You're right. That is stone-cold."

"More like frigid," Ginger corrected her.

Laura thought of Avery defending her to Jo Lynn at the party, when she'd never seen him step up like that before, not for her. "Sometimes people make mistakes," she said. "They can change if they want to."

"Please." Ginger picked at some lint on her skirt. "He can go screw himself as far as I'm concerned."

"Has he tried to call?"

"Only, like, a hundred times."

"Did you answer?"

"Of course not." Ginger crossed her arms, looking tough and wounded at the same time.

"Even though he was wrong, maybe he thought he was doing it for all the right reasons," Laura said, because she couldn't help herself; she didn't like seeing marshmallow-hearted Ginger so bitter about Javier and what he'd done. "Please, don't turn into an emotional hard-ass like Mac's always trying to be and write this dude off as fast as that. Do you think you'll ever see him again?"

"Yes . . . no . . . maybe . . . I don't know. Oh, God, I feel so totally lame." Ginger dropped her head back and rolled it against the headrest. "I haven't even talked to Mac since it happened. I can already hear her saying 'I told you so.' That's why I called you for a ride. I didn't need a third lecture about what a loser I am when it comes to boys. If Mac had her way, we'd all be entering a convent after high school." Ginger shook her head. "Okay, a little extreme, but you know what I mean."

"She's definitely the Uptight Musketeer," Laura agreed, though she knew a lot of Mac's fears and defensive behavior were tied to Jeanie Mackenzie's death. "But maybe we should cut her some slack. I mean, her dad married Honey Potts not that long after she lost her mom. Mac's trying so hard to protect her own emotions that I think it spills over to us sometimes. She doesn't want us getting hurt."

"You may be right," Ginger agreed, then went on to explain, "but I hate it when she acts disapproving, especially when it comes to my picking the wrong guys. She might not mean to come down hard, but she can."

Laura glanced sideways at her. "You weren't afraid to talk to me, though."

"Are you kidding?" Ginger snorted indelicately. "I knew you'd totally understand."

"I'm no Mac, that's for sure," Laura remarked. "I guess I'd rather get my heart broken than never let myself feel anything at all."

"Amen to that."

They were inching closer to the campus of PFP every minute, and Laura could see cars unloading girls of various heights and ages, so that it looked like an army of females in plaid skirts and white shirts swarmed the sidewalks and grassy yard between the redbrick buildings.

Laura swallowed the lump in her throat, tightening her hold on the steering wheel the nearer they got. The butterflies went wild in her belly as her nerves did somersault after somersault. Her gaze darted right and left, seeking Jo Lynn's shiny Audi, praying she'd luck out and miss running into her all day. Though that would be tricky, considering they only had thirty girls in their whole senior class. Laura figured that with her luck, she'd end up having several courses with the Queen of Mean. God forbid. How the hell could she handle that?

I will survive, she told herself, inventing another mantra. *I will rise up and stand strong against my enemy.*

Who was she kidding? A vengeful Jo Lynn Bidwell would frighten the pants off the Angel of Death.

"Have you got any Tums?" she asked Ginger, feeling decidedly queasy.

"Girlfriend, I've been sucking down Pepto all morning. You want the bottle?"

"Please."

While Ginger rummaged around in her bag, Laura pulled the car into the semicircular drive in front of the school, heading for the senior parking lot—which was when she spotted the burnt orange Corvette idling near the sidewalk drop-off.

Her heart leapt in her chest.

Avery is here?

Had he come to see her, maybe wish her good luck on her first day back before he headed over to Caldwell? Well, he'd shown up at Hobby on Saturday, so it wasn't that far-fetched, was it?

Grinning with anticipation, she edged her Mercedes ahead, slowed by the barely moving parade of vehicles in front of them, hoping she could pull up alongside him so she could lay on her horn and let him know she was there.

"Isn't that the Ratfink?" Ginger asked, handing over the pink Pepto-Bismol bottle, which Laura stuck in her lap between her thighs.

"Looks like it," Laura said gleefully, but her hopeful smile died as the passenger door of the 'Vette flew open and none other than Camie Lindell emerged. The skinny brunette leaned back inside the car for a lingering moment before she shut the door and scooted off.

"Oh, hell," Ginger said, exactly what Laura was thinking. "Are you okay, sweetie? You're awfully pale all of a sudden. Seriously, are you breathing?"

"I don't know," Laura got out in a strangled voice.

Was it possible to breathe with a knife stuck straight in your heart?

The Escalade directly ahead of her moved forward, giving Laura enough space to surge forward in the Roadster, coming up right alongside the Corvette and boxing it in. "Are you insane?" Ginger asked as Laura threw her car into park and unlocked the doors. "I know what you're thinking, but it's not a good time for a public smackdown. You've gotta resist the urge."

But Laura wasn't listening. She had her seat belt off in a flash, grabbed the Pepto, opened the door, and scrambled out of the Mercedes as fast as she could, striding around its hood and marching straight up to the driver's-side door of Avery's sports car. Horns honked all around her, and someone shouted, "Hey, don't hold the line up!" But she didn't care. It was all she could do to keep breathing as she rapped on the window and Avery slowly rolled it down.

"Laura, hey," he said, looking surprised. "You know, I meant to call you yesterday, but I kinda got tied up."

"Tied up, huh?" She leaned down so they were eye to eye. "Did you make Camie Lindell wear her mother's deb gloves too?"

"What?" His face clouded over. "You've got it all wrong. Camie called, she was upset, and—"

"Doesn't all this screwing around give you a guilty conscience?" Laura cut him off, hardly able to hold back her angry tears. "Or maybe heartburn?" she said, her hands shaking as she took the lid off the Pepto and dumped the slimy pink contents of the bottle right into his lap.

"Jesus, Laura! What's the matter with you?"

But she didn't stick around to chat. She hauled ass back to her car, figuring he had nothing to say—or yell—that she'd want to hear. All she knew for sure was that she'd given him all she had and he'd tossed it back in her face again.

"My God, are you okay?" Ginger asked the minute she got back behind the wheel of her Merc. "What happened?"

"I let Avery have your Pepto."

"You let him have it?"

"Yeah, all over his crotch." Laura's hands were still shaking as she took the wheel again, shifting back into gear and lurching ahead in the line, finally able to get around the drop-off lane and enter the senior lot.

"You didn't?" Ginger asked, and started to giggle when Laura nodded. Maybe someday, when she looked back on this moment, she'd laugh about it, too. But not now. All she felt was burned.

It is said that nothing
gives a brighter glow to the complexion,
or makes the eyes of a beautiful woman
sparkle so intensely, as triumph over another.
—Lady Caroline Lamb

Pick on me and that's between us.
Pick on my friends
and you've got a war on your hands.
—Mac Mackenzie

Fourteen

"*Mah-chelle!* Didn't you hear Alex honk his horn? You'd better dance fast, sister, or you're gonna be late!"

Mac ignored Honey's shrill cries, as, yes, she'd heard the horn and was moving as fast as she could. Was it her fault her alarm clock had decided to flake out on this particular morning? If Honey hadn't banged on her door twenty minutes ago, she would've slept through half the day. Not that she was going to thank her daddy's trophy wife for doing her any favors.

Mac's hair was still damp, the dark waves just beginning to curl. She'd barely had time to swipe her lips with gloss and brush a quick coat of mascara on her lashes so her eyes didn't disappear entirely behind her black-framed glasses. There was a strange crease down the back of her white oxford, which she hadn't noticed before; and it seemed like her plaid skirt was shorter than last year's model. It looked like something Burberry had left over from Christina Aguilera's *Stripped* tour. Okay, maybe it wasn't *quite* that small, but Mac felt like her hem was higher than it should be, leaving at least an inch of her knobby knees exposed.

She discarded a pair of black tights with a run up the back

and opted for white socks instead, quickly pulling on a fresh pair, and then slipped her feet into her beat-up black Coach loafers.

Ta-da. She was ready to go.

"Mah-chelle Mackenzie! Get your butt on down here now!"

Mac grabbed her black REI knapsack and ran down the stairs as fast as she could.

The stepmonster was standing at the bottom in her fuzzy robe and slippers, hair in rollers as big as orange-juice cans.

"Did my dad leave already?" Mac asked her, and Honey gave an irritated nod.

"He left a good twenty minutes ago. You're the one runnin' behind. You didn't have time to eat, did you? Take these," she said, and shoved a foil-wrapped pair of Pop-Tarts into Mac's hand.

Ah, nothing like a home-cooked breakfast to start the first day of my senior year at PFP off just right, Mac thought. "Thanks," she murmured before stuffing the cold toaster pastries into her bag.

"So you didn't see the morning paper either, did you?" Honey asked, to which Mac was tempted to reply, *Duh.* She'd only just come downstairs, after all. Honey's pink-nailed hand tapped a folded copy of the *Chronicle,* which she pulled out from under her arm. "Looks like Miss Ginger's been thrown into the fishbowl–"

"Yeah, I saw it on TV," Mac said sharply, cutting off further comment. Mac didn't want to discuss Ginger, particularly when she was still upset that the calls and texts and e-mails she'd sent to Ginger after watching the ten o'clock news had gone unanswered. Her BFF probably thought she'd get bawled out for being duped by that jerk Javier, and she was probably right. It was hard for Mac to see her friends get hurt by guy after guy after guy, and Mac was no good at biting her tongue.

With a hasty goodbye, she flung herself out the door and practically ran into Honey's BMW, which was parked right in front. She skirted it and hurried over to the gray Saab that sat farther up the driveway, its motor humming. Mac opened the car door, said, "Hi, Alex," and then tossed her knapsack in back before she got in.

"Mornin', sunshine," he said, and glanced at her with his hair falling onto his brow.

She almost did a double take, even though she'd seen him yesterday afternoon. She thought again how much less nerdlike he looked with the cool thin-rimmed specs, the longer hair, and the more confident way he held his newly six-foot-tall self. The way he squared his slim shoulders even made him look taller sitting behind the wheel. The only thing remotely geeky about his appearance now was his Caldwell uniform of white shirt, brown leather belt, and tan pants.

"You ready for it to start all over again?" he said.

She knew what he meant by "it": first-day angst, empty notebooks with so many lines to fill, new teachers to get used to, new and old faces to see, names to recall, and everyone dividing up into little cliques.

Her smart-ass answer: "Do I have a choice?"

"Nope."

"I didn't think so." She sighed and rested her head against the window as they pulled out of their street onto Knipp and veered left toward Taylorcrest.

Mac wondered how Ginger was doing and was anxious

to see her, even if her friend didn't want to talk about what happened yet. Mac made herself promise not to deliver any "I told you so's" when that was the last thing Ging probably wanted to hear.

"Do y'all have an assembly this morning?" Alex asked, breaking into her thoughts. "You think they could come up with something new instead of always doing the same old thing."

"Yeah, we've got one before first period," she told him, and glanced at the car's clock, knowing she'd have to scramble to get into the auditorium on time. Upper levels had their assembly before the middle grades.

"Too bad I can't be there to keep you awake, 'cuz I could do this," he said, and reached over to pinch the exposed skin of her thigh.

"Alex!" Mac blushed and hastily tugged the hem of her skirt closer to her knees.

"Sorry." He pulled his hand away and set it on the steering wheel, focusing on the road ahead and simply driving.

Within minutes, they were mere blocks away from the PFP campus, but the traffic had already slowed to a crawl. Mac let her gaze wander across the lines of high wooden fences that hid gracious houses and yards beyond the grass-lined ditches on either side of the road. The second Alex was able to pull the car into the crowded circle in front of Pine Forest's main building, Mac hopped out, retrieved her knapsack, slipped one arm through it, and hoisted it on her back.

"Thanks for the ride," she leaned in to tell him. "But I've gotta run."

"See you later," he said, adding, "You need a ride home? Unless you'd rather have one of your friends take you—"

But Mac had already slammed the door.

Cars and people swarmed the tiny campus, and she made her way through the throngs as best she could, ultimately getting sucked into the river of PFP zombies in white shirts and plaid skirts who flowed in a solid stream toward the doors.

Hitching her bag higher up on her shoulder, Mac headed as fast as she could up the stone steps and into the nearest of the neat brick buildings with their neoclassical façades and path-crossed courtyard meant to conjure up images of New England and the Ivy League. Trustees had spent a lot of money making sure real ivy grew up the red brick walls, though Mac had heard it was Algerian ivy, not English. Even the school's motto was intended to suggest deep roots and lofty aspirations: *Via, Veritas, Vita.*

"The Way, the Truth, the Life," strictly translated, though students through the years had corrupted the message, substituting "The Lays, the Booze, the Lies."

The "lays" and the "lies" seemed especially appropriate at the moment, Mac decided as she hurried through the hallways toward the auditorium, where the headmistress would deliver her annual "Welcome back, Pine Foresters" monologue, or so decreed the letter sent around to all parents and students several weeks earlier.

Ho-hum. Mac just hoped she could stay awake through the always-endless fifteen minutes.

When she flung open the doors to the foyer of the auditorium, the noise of a hundred and twenty voices buzzing in conversation stopped her dead in her tracks, as did the sea of heads and white shoulders yawning before her.

How am I supposed to find Laura and Ginger in this mob?

Forget about it.

Mac knew she'd have to wait until she got inside and found the seats for the senior class.

"Hey, Mac," said a voice from behind her. "How'd your summer go?"

It was the new girl who'd started in the middle of last spring's session: Cindy Chow, a transfer from St. John's across town. With her shiny black hair and striking Asian features, she definitely stood out from the usual cast of WASPs at PFP. She was both pretty and skinny enough to rate a membership in the Bimbo Cartel, but she seemed to like her independence. Mac had heard she rode a Harley, which wasn't exactly de rigueur in the Villages and probably defied a noise ordinance or two.

"I'm Cindy," she reminded Mac.

"I remember," Mac told her, and Cindy smiled, revealing tiny rows of straight white teeth.

"Hey, mind if I tag along?" Cindy asked. "I think I know where I'm going, but I'm still a little fuzzy on everything."

"Yeah, sure, follow me," Mac said as they merged into the crush of plaid-skirted, button-downed bodies.

A sign on the doors reminded them to PLEASE TURN OFF ALL ELECTRONIC DEVICES BEFORE ENTERING, so Mac shut off her cell and stuck it back in her bag.

"Have you seen Laura Bell or Ginger Fore?" she shot over her shoulder as Cindy followed her down the left-hand aisle.

"I don't think so, no. Oh, wow, I hope Ginger's okay. I saw the thing on the news about the tree protest. Did she get arrested for real?"

"No, I don't think so," Mac said, wishing she'd gleaned what she knew first-hand instead of from the TV. And she would have if Ginger hadn't been avoiding her. Well, her friend would have to face her soon enough, right?

"Well, I admire her guts," Cindy commented. "It can't have been easy chaining herself to a tree that her father's company planned to squash."

Mac felt yet another stab of guilt for not being more supportive when Ginger had told her what she was up to. "No, it couldn't have been easy at all."

When she was finally far enough down the aisle to make out faces instead of just hair, she skimmed the rows of seniors to find Jo Lynn Bidwell and her toadies, Camie and Trisha, whispering and looking particularly smug. The Bimbo Cartel must've sensed Mac staring, and stopped whispering long enough to smile disingenuously at her.

Mac moved on to the next row, scanning another dozen seniors until she spotted Laura's pale gold hair and realized her friend had settled into the seat farthest away from Jo Lynn and her cohorts.

Though Mac willed her BFF to glance in her direction, she didn't. Laura kept her gaze trained on the stage, her back ramrod straight. *Is something wrong?* Mac wondered.

"Hey," Cindy said, and nudged her gently from behind. "They're about to start."

Mac looked toward the stage just in time to catch their headmistress, Dr. Esther Percy, striding toward the podium. A typically wrinkled gray suit enveloped her heavyset body, its charcoal hue matching her short cap of gray hair almost precisely. Even from where she stood, Mac could make out the lines carved into Dr. Percy's face.

Cindy whispered, "The Seal. That's her nickname, right?"

Mac had to bite her lip to keep from laughing. "No, she's the Walrus," Mac corrected.

"Ah, yeah, I see the resemblance," Cindy whispered back

just as Dr. Percy tapped the microphone with a finger, sending a buzzing noise through the auditorium.

"Take your seats, please, girls," the headmistress said, clapping her hands, as if that would make everyone move faster. "And don't forget to turn off your cell phones, iPhones, BlackBerrys, and whatever other new gadgets you've collected over the summer."

Mac slipped off her knapsack and set it at her feet before settling into an empty seat beside a brawny girl from the tennis team, with Cindy sliding in behind her. If she leaned forward and looked right, she could glimpse Laura, but she saw no sign of Ginger.

Dr. Percy stood at the podium onstage, holding on with both hands, and Mac found herself pondering the number of chins that wobbled beneath the headmistress's Jell-O–like jaw. *Five*, she counted.

Finally the noise in the auditorium grew more muffled as everyone finished filing in and a couple of teachers shut the doors.

"Good morning, students," Dr. Percy trilled with a grin, displaying an impressive set of horse-sized teeth. She actually looked pleased that school had resumed and hundreds of pampered girls were in her charge again. "There's a special announcement affecting the whole school, so we'll hear about that first, before the a cappella choir performs our school song. Afterward, I'll have a few more announcements before I send you off to your homerooms. So let's get started"—she paused, turning stage right and gesturing—"come forward, Ms. Fore, and don't be shy."

From behind the folds of green curtains walked Ginger, her red hair tamed from its usual spikes, her white oxford shirt crisp, her skirt hovering at her kneecaps and no higher, wearing relatively staid stack-heeled Mary Janes with preppy socks. She seemed a bit pale, but other than that she appeared the model Pine Forest preppie, all shiny and scrubbed.

Mac nearly fell out of her seat.

What is Ginger doing up there? And why does she look like a Stepford schoolgirl instead of like herself?

"Ginger Fore, one of the more, er, socially conscious girls in our new senior class, has a few words she'd like to share with everyone," Dr. Percy proclaimed before turning over the mike, which Ginger reluctantly approached.

"Um, hello, everyone," she began, a bit shaky at first. "As some of y'all might know, I was involved in a protest this past weekend to save the Sam Houston Oak in Bunker Hill Park, only it kind of ended badly"—there was a smattering of laughter, though Ginger seemed unfazed—"and I'm truly sorry if my actions embarrassed the school or my family. I thought I was doing something good, and still believe that I was."

Oh, man, it's no wonder Ginger was too embarrassed to talk to me, Mac realized. It was obviously too humiliating to explain that she'd been forced to make a public apology at the assembly.

"At the time, I didn't know it was my father who'd donated the land to Pine Forest so the school could enlarge the parking lot, but I learned that fast enough last night." Ginger hesitated, and Mac could see the slip of paper tremble in her hands. "I discussed the whole thing with my dad in private, and he spoke with the school's trustees, who've agreed to spare the tree and build the parking lot around it.

199

My father's company will also match the funds the school has been raising to build a new library, and they'll donate new computers for the student study area." Ginger glanced aside at Dr. Percy, who gave a hearty nod. "I guess that's it, then. Thank you for listening, and, um, welcome back."

The murmur of voices rippled through the audience, and several people applauded, though most seemed unsure of how exactly to respond.

The headmistress resumed her place at the microphone and thanked Ginger, who was already halfway across the stage.

"Loser," Mac heard someone cough before Ginger disappeared behind the folds of green curtain. She glanced over her shoulder to find Jo Lynn, Camie, and Trisha smirking.

"Now will everyone please rise and join the choir in singing the PFP spirit song," Dr. Percy said as the podium became engulfed in a semicircle of a dozen girls in white shirts and plaid skirts.

Mac rose to her feet, and the auditorium filled with a noise akin to an elephant stampede as the rest of the upper grades did too.

After a sadly off-key rendition of "All Hail, Pine Forest Prep" and a smattering of first-day announcements, the room quickly emptied. Mac grabbed her bag from her feet and pushed her way past Cindy Chow, muttering a hasty "Excuse me." Then she took off, hurrying up the aisle, her knapsack slapping against her back as she went after Laura, who'd seemingly disappeared into thin air.

Mac ended up finally catching Laura at her locker. "Hey, Laura!" she said, slightly out of breath, as she leaned in front of her own locker, just a few doors down. "I feel like you and Ging are both avoiding me—"

"Sorry, Mac," Laura said quietly, head down as she worked the combination on her lock. "I've got a lot on my mind, and Ginger's just afraid you'll get on her case."

"I know, I know." Mac thought her friend looked on the pale side, like maybe she was coming down with something. Or maybe she was just holding something in, like whatever had happened during her disappearing act from the sleepover on Saturday night. "You okay?"

"I'm fine."

Mac didn't believe her for a minute. She stood and watched Laura jerk open her locker door, ready to shove her book bag in. Then Laura hesitated and reached inside for something that looked like a flyer. As she read it, she turned even paler before she crumpled up the sheet and shoved it back in, shutting her locker with a bang.

"*Shit*," Laura whispered, leaning her head against the metal. "It can't believe this is happening."

"What's happening?" Mac felt as out of the loop as she ever had. Why was she always the last to know everything? "What's going on?"

"I can't talk now. I'll tell you at lunch," Laura whispered, before grabbing Mac's arm and saying, "Let's go off campus, just you, me, and Ginger. No more secrets, okay?"

"Okay," Mac said as Laura nodded and glanced nervously around them before spotting something over Mac's shoulder that made her freeze. Abruptly, she took off the other way.

What the hell was that about?

Did it have to do with Avery? He was so totally a Ratfink.

"Oh, wow, I'm *so* sorry."

Someone bumped into Mac's arm, and she looked up to find herself face to face with Jo Lynn Bidwell.

"My heavens, did I knock into you? How clumsy of me. I guess I was just preoccupied watching your large friend run off like a frightened rabbit. Did she find something scary in her locker?"

Mac stood stock-still, pressing her sweat-dampened palms against her thighs, but she said nothing, having learned long ago that it was far simpler to ignore than to engage a Bimbo.

"Um, just a little tip, girl-to-girl, Mackenzie. You have some weird wrinkle goin' up the back of your shirt," Jo Lynn drawled, as Camie and Trisha stood behind her giggling. "What's the problem, Bookworm? Can't your new mom use an iron?"

And just like that, the three of them glided off.

Mac glared at their retreating backs, trying hard to breathe evenly and not go after them shouting, *At least my daddy didn't buy me boobs for my sixteenth birthday!*

Something about the three of them scared the hell out of her.

And she had a very strong feeling the Bimbo Cartel had scared Laura, too.

Life's a bitch and then they call you one.
—Mary Frances Connelly

It's impossible to fight
fair against someone who plays dirty.
—Ginger Fore

Fifteen

Ginger toyed with the salad she'd ordered, her appetite non-existent. And it wasn't the fault of La Fiesta, a favorite hole-in-the-wall Mexican restaurant at Bunker Hill and Katy Freeway that she, Mac, and Laura had slipped off to during their lunch break. Even Mac and Laura couldn't seem to do more than pick at the gooey cheese enchiladas on their plates, and usually they demolished them in a few breathless minutes.

Ginger thought her two best friends looked as wrung out as she felt after discussing all the gory details of her crush on Javier Garcia with them, from the moment she'd met him until the "tree fiasco," as Mac called it.

She abandoned any pretense at eating when her cell started ringing, and she snatched it from her bag only to realize it was Javier again. She sighed loudly, holding her Razr up. "So should I answer him or not?"

"No," Mac insisted, just as Laura barked, "Yes!"

Ginger stared at the phone, letting it ring a second time and then a third, until Laura jumped up from her seat, muttered, "Oh, for God's sake," snatched the cell from Ginger's hand, and answered it herself: "Javier? Yeah,

Ginger's here, and I'll let you talk to her in a sec. But if you hurt her again, I will personally hunt you down and kill you, you got that?"

"Give me that!" Ginger grabbed her Razr back and put it to her ear, hesitantly saying, "Hey, it's me."

"Are you okay?" he asked, such worry in his voice that the icy wall she'd put up threatened to melt.

"I'm fine," she told him as Mac and Laura looked on, "but I can't really talk."

"*Su amigas* . . . your friends are there?"

"Yes."

"Can I see you later, then? We could meet—" he suggested, but Ginger cut him off.

"No," she said. Seeing him when she felt so confused by what he'd done would just make her feel worse. She needed time to sort things out, to decide whether what he'd done was pardonworthy. "I'm grounded," she told him, "and Deena's watching me like a hawk."

"Give me a chance to explain so you'll understand," he said, sounding almost desperate.

Ginger turned a shoulder to her friends, who suddenly feigned interest in their food, though she knew they were listening to every word. "Maybe someday, if I ever stop being pissed at you."

She hung up then before he could confuse her further by trying to sweet-talk her out of being angry. She felt a nudge against her shin and realized it was Mac's foot.

"You did good," Mac said. "You feeling all right?"

Ginger sighed. "Remember that day in gym class when Coach Nadine made us do, like, fifty jumping jacks right after lunch and I threw up?"

"Yeah"—Mac made a face—"you tossed your cookies on my brand-new Skechers."

"Well, I feel just like that right now," Ginger said, then turned on Laura. "How could you do that? You knew I didn't want to talk to him!"

But Laura didn't appear to hear. She seemed engrossed in pushing a spoon around the goo of melted cheese on her platter.

"Laura?" Ginger tried again, suddenly feeling less angry and more worried. "Earth to Laura Bell!"

Finally, Mac leaned over to poke Laura in the shoulder.

"Huh?" Laura glanced up from her food, clearly a million miles away.

"What the hell is up with you?" Ginger asked, noticing then how shiny with sweat Laura's face was, and how her friend kept biting her bottom lip. "You look really freaked out about something. Is it Avery?" she asked.

Laura shook her head. "It's Jo Lynn Bidwell."

At the mention of Jo Lynn's name, Mac practically leapt out of her seat. "Oh, my God, y'all," she blurted out. "I completely forgot to tell you! Jo-L bumped smack into *me* while I was standing at my locker. She *totally* did it on purpose, I'm sure of it. That girl never does anything without an agenda."

Laura's eyes went wide as quarters.

Mac settled back in her chair, her cheeks an angry pink. "The witch asked if you'd found something scary in your locker, Laura, and then she made a snarky remark about the back of my shirt having a crease. Is it completely evil of me to imagine how nice it would be if someone ran over all three Bimbos with a Hummer? It's disgusting how they get their kicks by putting other people down—"

"Or going all-out to destroy them," Ginger butted in, because ragging on the Bimbo Cartel was one of her favorite pastimes. "Remember the photos of Jennifer Howland they put up on Facebook? The ones from her New Year's party where she was flashing her boobs and acting all lesbo with some girl from Stratford? Didn't she end up moving or something, she was so humiliated?"

"I think everyone in Texas saw those pics, so she had nowhere to run but out of the state," Mac was saying when Laura bolted out of her seat, jarring the table so hard that the plates and utensils rattled. Water slopped out of Ginger's glass onto the table in front of her.

"Hey," she said, "careful!"

"I think I'm going to be sick." Laura put a hand to her mouth and made a run for the ladies' room.

"Something's seriously wrong," Mac said as they watched Laura's departing back, and Ginger couldn't have agreed more.

"I hope it's nothing to do with her run-in with Avery this morning," Ginger voiced her thoughts aloud.

"What?" Mac looked ready to choke.

"The Ratfink was dropping off Camie Lindell."

"Oh, God," Mac moaned. "The dude needs to be shot."

"My thoughts exactly. C'mon, let's go."

Their chairs noisily scraped the floor as they got up, Ginger leading the way to the bathroom, pushing open the door with a creak, and finding Laura standing at the mirror, hands braced on the edge of the sink. Her chest heaved, sobs catching in her throat, and she swiped at her eyes with her sleeve.

"Laura," Ginger called out, rushing to her side and

putting a hand on her arm as Mac did the same. "What's got you so messed up?"

She nearly said *No secrets,* but she realized she'd broken that rule too many times already. It would have been hypocritical to chastise Laura for doing it too.

"I'm totally screwed." Laura sighed and tears slipped down her pale cheeks, even as she closed her eyes to stop them. "It's starting all over again, just when I thought I'd gotten over it. That I'd cried enough. It's like them turning on me a year ago, when they didn't think I was good enough to be with Avery, and now they're after me again, right before D-Day, so they can keep me off the Glass Slipper Club's list."

"A year ago," Ginger repeated, shaking her head. "Look, I don't know what happened back then, or how they hurt you, but the Bimbo Cartel can't keep you from being a Rosebud. They don't have the power. Your mother's buds with Bootsie. Even Jo Lynn couldn't make up a lie big enough to run you off."

"What if it's not a lie?" Laura whispered, reaching up to wipe her cheeks, adding hoarsely, "What if Jo Lynn has pictures?"

Ginger looked over at Mac, who shrugged.

"Pictures of what?" she asked, wondering what Jo Lynn Bidwell could possibly be holding over Laura's head.

Laura exhaled, drying the tears from her cheeks with the white sleeve of her button-down. "You have to understand something first," she slowly began. "Jo and Camie and Trisha . . . they pretended to be my friends, you know, even when something deep inside told me to watch out for them. But Avery hangs with that crowd, and he trusts them. I fell right into their trap. *Stupid, stupid, stupid.*" She leaned forward, gently knocking her forehead on the mirrored glass until Ginger stopped her. "Jo Lynn had a sleepover one night last summer. Her parents were gone, and I got really drunk. I passed out at some point, and when I woke up"—she hesitated, her chin trembling, and wet her lips—"my clothes were gone. Someone had written all over my body with a laundry marker. *Slut, whore, pig, fat-ass,* ugly things." She sniffled, and Ginger snatched a paper towel from the dispenser, handing it over so Laura could wipe her nose. "The words were on my arms, my legs, my stomach, my breasts. It took a week for it all to wash off, and I was too horrified to tell anyone, so I kept it to myself and I prayed it would all go away. I thought it had."

"Well, hell, Laura," Mac said angrily. "You should've told us. We could've helped you kick their asses, or called the cops. Isn't that like assault or something? Was Avery involved in this?"

Laura shook her head. "No, he wasn't there. It was just the three of them, though I know Jo Lynn was behind it. It was her twisted way of telling me I wasn't one of them and I never had been."

"What about the photos?" Ginger was hardly able to digest what Laura had been through and was unable to fathom how someone could treat another human being like that.

"Jo Lynn took them," Laura said, voice warbling, sounding ashamed all over again. "She e-mailed them the next day and told me to keep my fat mouth shut or I'd be sorry. She wanted me to stay away from Avery, and I know she said something to him, because he stopped coming around. I couldn't have faced him anyway after that, but I'd hoped he'd . . . well, I was a fool."

"That flyer in your locker–" Mac started, but Laura ran right over her, obviously desperate to finally talk.

"It wasn't a flyer. It was one of the pictures, printed out on regular paper. But there was no warning this time, not a written one, anyway. Nothing. I couldn't even prove it was Jo Lynn who put it there, but I know what it means. She's going to use it to keep me from being a Rosebud, and not even Tincy's friendship with Bootsie will be able to stop it. And she knows I can't fight back." Tears pooled on Laura's dark lashes. "What if my mom sees those pictures, or my dad? Or the whole school, for that matter?" Laura turned to Ginger with a mascara-smeared face. "I'm dead, aren't I? If only I'd stayed away from Avery . . . if I hadn't crashed Jo Lynn's party on Saturday night just to see him–"

"*That's* where you were?" Mac blurted out, looking ready to lecture, until Ginger said, "*Not now.*"

Laura sniffed and glanced in the mirror again, using her pinky finger to try to repair her smudged eyes. "Too bad the Donald Trump of H-town can't buy my way out of this mess, huh, Ging? Old Harry Bell could offer the Glass Slipper Club a huge honking donation, and it wouldn't be the same. Running a company that sells plumbing parts to the whole freaking world might bring in the cash, but it doesn't have the same cachet, if you know what I mean."

Ginger flinched as she took the jab, telling herself that Laura was too frightened and angry to realize what she was saying. Still, it stung, and she couldn't help the sarcasm that slipped into her voice as she said, "Sorry my dad can't come to your rescue, Laura, but if I can do anything, I will."

"Me too," Mac offered. "There's got to be some way to

stop the Bimbo Cartel. Anyone know where I can buy Bimbo remover? Hey, I could use that at home to get rid of Honey, too."

"Bimbo remover . . . Honey . . . oh, God, wait a minute." Laura paused, blinking rapidly, like a thousand lightbulbs were going off in her head. Without warning, she snagged Mac's arm, asking her, "Wasn't your stepmom a beauty queen? Didn't she do the circuit for, like, most of her life until she met your dad?"

"I guess she did, but what does that have to do with–" Mac wasn't able to complete the sentence.

"She's not that much older than we are, is she?" Laura said, obviously thinking out loud. "Which means she may have known Jo Lynn on the pageant scene, and Jo Lynn was always bragging about how she took the front-runners down so she could get the crown. Maybe Honey knows some really ugly skeletons Jo Lynn has in her closet along with all those beaded dresses and sparkly tiaras. Or she could even make something up, for all I care. Whatever it takes to make the bitch back down."

Mac looked stone-faced. "What exactly are you suggesting?"

"I have an idea that might work if you'll do it," Laura told her.

"Do what?" Mac shifted on her feet.

Laura cleared her throat, but it was still scratchy as she said quietly, "You have to ask Honey Potts to help me."

Behind her smart-girl glasses, Mac's eyes seemed about to pop out. "You want me to ask for a favor from the Trophy Wife? Are you out of your frickin' mind?"

Ginger jumped on the idea. Anything was worth a shot.

"C'mon, Mac, it's not that big of a deal. You need to make nice with Honey sometime."

"Y'all are crazy."

Laura clasped her hands over her heart and pleaded. "I beg you, Mac. This can't wait. You have to talk to her right after school. The invitations could be going out any minute. I don't have time to waste." She caught Mac's hand on her left and Ginger's on her right, and she squeezed. "Being debs together, it's what we've talked about since we were kids. We're the Three Amigas, right? We can't let the Bimbo Cartel break that up. We just can't."

"All right, all right, all right," Mac agreed, "I'll give it a try, but I can't promise you anything. I have no clue what Honey knows about Jo Lynn, if anything. But I'm on your side, Laura, no matter what."

"Does that mean you'll go for it, Mac? That you'll do the deb thing?" Ginger pressed, figuring that the heat was on. It was do or die, now or never, and any other cliché that applied.

Mac hesitated, first looking at Ginger and then at Laura. "Yeah, I'm in."

"All for one and one for all, isn't that how it goes?" Ginger said, a strange mix of anxiety and excitement coursing through her.

"Maybe our motto should be more like 'Bomb the Bimbo Cartel,'" Laura suggested, and Mac remarked, "It's got a nice ring to it."

"I'm in," Ginger said.

Mac added, "Ditto."

"*That's* what I'm talkin' 'bout!"

Laura pulled them all together in a group hug, and they

held on tight until Laura started giggling, her shoulders shaking contagiously, and pretty soon Ginger and Mac were laughing like idiots too. It was one of those spontaneous moments that bonded them stronger than glue, and Ginger found herself wishing it could last forever.

I hate to spread rumors—
but what else can one do with them?
—Amanda Lear

Never turn your back on an enemy,
even when you think you've got her crushed.
—Jo Lynn Bidwell

Sixteen

"Yes, yes, I'm horrified too!" Bootsie Bidwell exclaimed into her cell as she paced the marble-tiled foyer, unaware that Jo Lynn was eavesdropping from behind the banister on the curve of the stairwell. "I don't know who's behind that awful photo, but I agree that we need to discuss it. I've called a special meeting of the selection committee for five o'clock, here at the house. All right, Millicent, I'll see you soon."

Jo Lynn held her breath for an instant, hoping her mother wouldn't head upstairs.

"Nan, for heaven's sake, where are you?" Bootsie called for the housekeeper, and the heels of her Marc Jacobs pumps clicked across the floor as she disappeared en route to the kitchen.

Jo Lynn sighed and hugged her knees to her chest, smiling and feeling as if she owned the world, or at least her part of it. God, how she loved it when things went according to plan.

I don't know who's behind that awful photo, her mother had proclaimed, but Jo Lynn knew who'd done it. *Me, myself, and I,* she thought. She'd known those revealing photos she'd taken of a passed-out-drunk Laura last summer would come in handy someday, and not just to put an end to Avery and Laura's farce of a relationship. Jo hadn't exactly planned to use the images ever again, except as a threat to keep Laura in her place. Until the party-crashing Miss Bell had shown up at the guesthouse on Saturday night. Jo Lynn realized then that it was time to play for keeps.

So she'd arranged for the worst of the photographs to be privately couriered to each member of the Rosebud selection committee—in unmarked envelopes with no return address, of course—and she'd paid cash so there would be no way to trace her. When she'd arrived home from school, Bootsie had already been in a tizzy, fielding phone calls and returning others, scheduling the last-minute confab to decide Laura's fate.

"I thought we had the list settled too," she'd heard her mother tell one of her GSC cronies. "But I guess we'll have to reconsider. We can't have obscene photos of a Rosebud floating around, now, can we?"

Jo Lynn rose to her feet, sliding a hand down the banister as she descended to the first floor, thinking she'd done her mother proud, even if Bootsie was unaware of what she'd done, as Mommy Dearest had forever lectured her about knowing her competition and playing on their weaknesses. Jo Lynn had won more beauty pageants than she could count because of that advice. There was a lot to be said for striking first, and it had earned her more titles than she would've had if she'd sat back and twiddled her thumbs. Winning had been everything then. Hell, it still was.

Taking advantage of Laura Bell had been almost too easy.

When the Swamp Donkey had dated Avery Dorman and weaseled her way into the A-list, Jo Lynn had quickly learned two things about her: the girl was head over heels in love with Avery (how clueless could she be?) *and* she'd kill to be a debutante.

So Jo was taking down Laura in two ways: one, distributing the photo to ensure that Laura's name wouldn't be anywhere on the list of ten Rosebuds-to-be, and two, writing the script that had Camie begging a ride to school from Avery so that Laura could watch and weep.

If *that* hadn't doused any fire that had been rekindled between the debu-skank and Avery, Jo Lynn wasn't sure what would.

The doorbell rang, knocking the smile from Jo Lynn's face.

"I'll get it," she shouted instinctively, because she was standing right there, at the foot of the stairwell, her hand on the balustrade.

She walked barefoot across the rosa aurora marble floor, hearing the grandfather clock chime the quarter hour as she passed. A glance at the ornate face told her it wasn't yet five. Had one of the GSC selection committee members shown up a tad early?

She peered through the peephole and spied Dillon standing on the doorstep. He wore an Astros cap, and he kept thumbing the bill, looking nervous.

Her heart did a little two-step at the sight of him, and she hurriedly unlocked the dead bolt to let him in.

"Hey," she said, and he gave her an anxious smile. "You want to come inside?" She gestured back at the foyer, but he shook his head.

"I can't stay, but I wanted to come by and apologize in person," he told her, "for leaving you high and dry on Saturday night. It's just that something came up." He shifted on his feet. "A friend of mine, well, he got really drunk, and—"

"You had to go take care of things," she finished for him, figuring it was something like that. Dillon was so generous, way too big-hearted for his own good. People tended to take advantage of him, and it crazed Jo Lynn when he let them do it. "I'm just glad you're here," she told him, grinning like a fool as she reached for his hand. "I was worried about you. You should've called me back. Sometimes texting just isn't the same as talking."

"Forgive me?" he said, and his fingers wrapped tightly around hers. He pulled her into a bear hug, rocking her back and forth on the welcome mat.

Jo Lynn's answer was to tip her head so he could kiss her, which he did quite soundly, his lips firmly pressed against hers.

All too quickly, he drew away. "I've gotta go. Football practice calls," he said, and Jo Lynn nodded. "We'll go out soon, okay? You pick the place."

"Sounds perfect," she told him as he gave a wave and loped back to his Mustang. He had the top down, so she could see him climb inside and flip his ball cap backward before he gunned the engine and took off.

Jo touched a finger to her lips, still feeling his mouth on hers. The worry in her belly seemed to dissolve, and she grinned as she headed back inside and shut the door behind her.

Dillon's still mine, Laura Bell's about to get her big ass booted from the deb list, and all is right with the world, she thought as she strolled into the living room and plopped down on the chintz sofa. She picked up a copy of *Elle* from the coffee table and kept her eye on the front hallway.

It won't be long before the guillotine slices down on poor Laura's neck, she realized, and shivered with anticipation when the doorbell finally chimed at a few minutes till five. This time, she made no move to answer it, as her mother's high heels click-clacked in response.

Jo Lynn recognized Tincy Bell's voice the moment she heard her saying, "Bootsie, darlin', I flew all the way back from Telluride on Harry's jet after you phoned, and I raced over straight from the airport. What the hell's going on? You can't believe this garbage is real. Somebody's playin' us for fools. You know these kind of things can be done on computers. . . ."

"This way, Tincy, if you would, and we'll talk a moment privately before the meeting begins." Bootsie caught her friend's elbow and guided her in the other direction, away from Jo Lynn, toward the study, too far away for Jo to hear.

Within another ten minutes, the entire contingent had shown up, and Nanny Nan had them all sequestered in the dining room, or so Jo Lynn thought. Which was why it surprised her when the doorbell rang once more and the voice that declared, "Well, hey, there, I'm here for the meetin'," was one Jo Lynn didn't recognize.

"I truly need to speak with Miss Boots alone, please, before anything gets started," the clubber-come-lately insisted, and Jo Lynn set the *Elle* aside, wanting to see who the hell the woman was, because none of the regulars in the GSC would've ever called Bootsie "Miss Boots" without fearing reprisal.

"Tell her that Mrs. Daniel Mackenzie wants to have a word with her, and I think she'll appreciate hearin' me out."

Mrs. Daniel Mackenzie?

As in Mac Mackenzie's new mommy?

Jo Lynn knew nothing about the woman except what she'd read in the Society pages of the *Chronicle* before and after the shotgun wedding. Supposedly, the second Mrs. Mac had worn a tiara or two in her day, though Jo Lynn didn't remember any of the older crowd. It'd been difficult enough to keep tabs on the girls in her tier.

Maybe it was time to get properly introduced.

She got up from the sofa and strode into the front hallway, stopping just shy of where mousy Mac's new mummy stood tapping a toe on the floor impatiently.

"I'll take care of Mrs. Mackenzie, Nan," Jo said, and shooed away the housekeeper, who murmured something about fetching iced tea for the committee members already congregated.

Jo Lynn crossed her arms while Honey glanced above her at the two-story-high ceiling with its hand-painted mural depicting Michelangelo's masterpiece in the Sistine Chapel. A Venetian-glass chandelier dripped from its center.

"Nice place you have here. Very refined," Mrs. Mackenzie said, walking over to the Louis XIV bombé chest and running a finger over the art deco bronze atop it. "I'm redecorating a house myself, and it's not as easy as it seems."

"My mother has an interior designer from Paris."

"Is that so?" The woman finally stopped gawking and turned around, hands on hips, cocking her head and giving

Jo Lynn the once-over. "So you're the infamous Jo Lynn Bidwell, I take it."

"And you're the first Mrs. Mac's replacement," Jo replied, sizing up the trophy wife, from her retro blond flip to her vivid makeup and perfect posture. She noted the snug white cropped jeans that were clearly Juicy Couture and the black off-the-shoulder top that was most certainly Michael Kors. The red patent-leather pumps with the cutout toes had to be Miu Miu. "Wait a second," she said, thinking the woman looked awfully familiar somehow. "Were you the Miss Houston runner-up, like, five years ago?"

Mrs. Mackenzie turned, clearly looking amused. "I was Honey Potts back then, and I should've won, but my damned accordion blew a pleat." She put her hands on her hips, her chin jerking up. "Though I guess I could've stolen the title if I'd been a little more cunning. Like you, sweet pea."

Is the woman on drugs?

Jo Lynn sniffed. "What's *that* supposed to mean?"

Honey smiled, a perfect pageant grin, showing just the upper teeth, which were as straight and white as Chiclets.

"Oh, darlin', I think you know precisely what I'm talkin' about. I was still hangin' around the circuit when you were working the junior scene. I did makeup and clothes styling, and I even judged a little." She tapped a pink-painted fingernail against her dimpled chin. "You were such a single-minded thing, I'm sure you looked right through me then. But I'll never forget all the stories I heard about you and how something terrible always happened to the front-runner in all the pageants you won."

Jo Lynn's mouth went dry, and her heart started racing.

She wet her lips and managed to say, "Just what are you implying?"

"Oh, sister, I know you're not even close to stupid, so don't play dumb with me." Honey took a few steps closer, so that they were nearly nose to nose. "If you really want to stir up the pot, like you're doing with that poor Laura Bell—"

"I didn't do anything—" Jo Lynn started to deny the accusation, but Honey talked right over her.

"—then I can toss a whole lot more spice into the mix. Don't you think folks would love to put all the pieces together? I know more than a few girls out there who'd be interested to hear all about how you fixed near about every contest where you came out on top."

"You're crazy. I don't know what you're talking about," Jo Lynn snapped; she felt her armpits dampen, her palms get slick. "So why don't you just bounce, and I'll tell my mother you couldn't stay for the meeting."

"Bounce?" Thinly plucked brows shot up. "I don't think so, sugar. I came to share my own little bombshell with the committee. I mean, if you're aiming to get Laura Bell's name knocked off the deb list with a doctored-up picture—"

"It's not doctored!" Jo blurted out before she could stop herself.

Honey's plucked eyebrows arched. "I thought you didn't know what I was talkin' about?"

Jo Lynn grabbed the woman's arm. "Get out," she growled.

But Honey shook her off. "You remember Miss Teen Grand Prairie?" she started reeling off. "Seems she got a bad case of the runs after someone put stool softener in the brownies she found in her welcome basket. Poor girl couldn't leave the ladies' room long enough to sing 'Ave Maria' in the talent competition for Miss Teen Texas." The woman cocked her head. "With her out of the picture, your flaming baton routine put you in the lead. Funny how that worked out."

"Do I have to call the cops to get you to leave?" Jo Lynn said, looking around frantically. She had to get this woman out of there. Where had she put her cell?

"Oh, but I'm not finished with you yet." Honey shook her fluffy blond head. "And what about Miss Junior South Padre Island? Remember her? She had a terrible fear of spiders, and somehow a big ol' hairy tarantula from a local pet shop ended up in the poor thing's bed at the Marriott. She fainted dead away, chipped a tooth on the nightstand, and had to drop out of the contest altogether." The woman squinted at her. "Without Debra Jane in the swimsuit competition, you had it won hands down and took the crown. Is any of this ringin' any bells?"

Jo Lynn felt frozen to the marble floor. "This has to be a joke, right?"

"Sorry, sweet pea, but it's no joke." Honey paused and opened her black Prada hobo bag and pulled out a sheaf of folded papers. "Once I put out the word this afternoon to my old friends on the circuit, a whole slew of 'em sent me e-mails, swapping memories of you. Seems everyone has a story to tell, which made me got to thinkin' what might happen if they started comparing notes"—she blinked double time—"my oh my, but you'd be in deep doo-doo. You might have to return all your trophies and tiaras. I hope you haven't gotten *too* attached to 'em all."

Jo Lynn could hardly breathe. "You're bluffing," she got out, voice raspy. Even to her own ears, she sounded scared.

"Tit for tat, sweet pea," Honey said, more steel magnolia in her voice than sugar, and Jo could see in her face that she meant it.

Hell's bells! How did this bitch get on the selection committee? Or in the GSC, for that matter?

"You all right? You're lookin' a bit green around the gills."

Jo Lynn wanted to scream.

"Look, it's easy," Honey Mackenzie said softly. "Either you have a word with your momma, baby girl, or I will. Just tell her it was all a bad prank, and you're sorry. Then I'll shut my mouth and you won't hear from me again. But if you'd rather have your name smeared all over the history books of every pageant you've ever been in, well, that's your choice. And you've got five seconds to make it."

The woman paused and moved her mouth as she silently counted, *One, two, three, four, five.*

"Time's up, sweet pea, and I didn't hear you volunteer to confess to your mama. So if you'll excuse me, I've a meetin' to attend. I believe the housekeeper said the dining room was that-a-way." Honey brushed past Jo Lynn, who held her breath for a long moment before calling, *"Wait."*

Did this really just happen?

Jo Lynn had never *ever* been outmaneuvered like this. Nothing Bootsie had taught her had prepared her for getting outfoxed. She swallowed hard, tasting crow and wishing she could spit it out right on the second Mrs. Mackenzie's feet.

"I'll talk to Mother," she said glumly, giving in despite the way every fiber in her body resisted. She had no way to fight against Honey's threats. "I just need a minute, okay?"

What the hell was she going to say?

She'd have to lie through her teeth and blame someone else, because she couldn't very well tell Bootsie her plan to bring Laura down had been shot to hell by a has-been runner-up to Miss Houston. Bootsie had absolutely no tolerance for failure.

Shit.

Jo Lynn fumed as she reluctantly hunted down her mother. Someone was going to pay for this someday. And she knew just who that someone was.

Things are going to get a lot worse
before they get worse.
—Lily Tomlin

If being a deb isn't life or death,
why does it feel that way to me?
—Laura Bell

Seventeen

Laura sat on the edge of a chair in the den, waiting for the doorbell to ring, completely on edge. She hadn't been able to swallow a bite at dinner, and she'd managed to chew her nails down to the quick already. If she didn't hear the bell chime soon, her cuticles were next.

It wasn't even seven o'clock, but she'd already gotten word that the Rosebud invitations had gone out hours ago.

What if the Bimbo Cartel had succeeded and her worst fear came true? What would she do if no one came to the door at all?

Laura turned on the TV, then switched it off again. Even the noise couldn't drown out her gloomy mood.

Ginger had called half an hour ago to say her invitation had been delivered. "By a dude in white gloves, top hat, and tails," she'd gushed. "In some funky old car my mother said is a Bugatti. I'm sure yours will come soon."

Her cell suddenly vibrated against her thigh, and Laura snatched it open.

"Mine just showed up," Mac said, sounding awfully calm and cool, when Laura would have been busting a gut. "Any sign of yours?"

"No," Laura winced, "and I'm beginning to have my doubts."

"No worries, remember?" Mac tried to reassure her. "I told you what Honey said, that she scared the pants off Jo Lynn with some dirt from her pageant friends. By the time the committee meeting broke up last night, everyone was convinced the photographs were a prank. Honey swore that no one altered the list, and your name was there the last she'd seen."

"I hope you're right," Laura whispered, hardly knowing what to believe. All she could do was wait it out. In another hour or so, she'd know if she'd lost and Jo Lynn Bidwell had won. If that was the case, it was too unbearable to consider. She'd have to pack up and move to Burundi for sure.

"Call me when you get yours, okay?"

"Yeah," Laura said dully. Then she hung up and tossed the cell onto a nearby club chair. Tears threatened her eyes, but she made herself breathe slowly in and out. *I am who I am,* she kept telling herself, *and I will not fall apart.*

Tincy popped her head in. "You doing all right, sweetheart? Want some company?"

"Sure." Laura blinked the tears away, putting on a happy face so her mother wouldn't decide to give her a pep talk. Tincy had been so panicked when she'd heard about the obscene photo from Bootsie Bidwell that she'd jetted home from the cabin in Telluride and had been practically glued to Laura's side ever since.

Her mother settled down beside her. She was so tiny it was like a bird perching on a twig. The sofa cushion barely registered Tincy's weight as she crossed her thin legs and took Laura's large hand in her petite one. "Everything will be fine," her mom assured her, and Laura sighed.

"Can we talk about something else, please?"

"All right." Tincy tossed back her chocolate-brown hair streaked with copper, gazing at the den's fifteen-foot ceilings until she came up with a topic not off-limits. "Did I tell you how fit you're lookin', sweetheart? All that fresh air must've done you good."

"Yeah, terrific," Laura said, hoping her mother wouldn't get into her weight and how she was still the same size she'd been before she'd left.

Instead, Tincy went in another direction. "How's school goin' so far? You like your classes?"

Laura refrained from rolling her eyes. "It's only been two days, Mother. Ask me again in about a month."

If Tincy was annoyed by being put off, she didn't show it. "Well, okay then, how about boys?"

"What about them?"

"*Laura,*" Tincy drawled, and made a frustrated face, her powdered nose wrinkling. "You're not seeing that Dorman boy again, are you?"

Like Laura wanted to discuss Avery any more than she wanted to talk about her missing Rosebud invitation? *Not!*

"No," she said.

"Laura?" Her mother gave her that look, clearly disbelieving.

She half-turned on the sofa, staring Tincy straight in the eye and telling her pointedly, "No, ma'am, I am *not* seeing Avery Dorman at the moment."

It was the cold, hard truth. She hadn't seen him since her fateful run-in with him at PFP on Monday morning when he'd been giving his latest ho a ride to school. Laura hoped the Pepto-Bismol had left a pretty pink stain on his nicely pressed pants.

"Well, good," her mother declared, "because you're better off without him."

Whatever.

Tick, tick, tick.

The second hand on her Patek Philippe jogged around the face of her wristwatch, until Laura thought she might go mad.

And then it happened.

The doorbell chimed.

Laura popped out of her seat faster than an exploding bottle rocket.

"Sweetheart, for heaven's sake," Tincy sputtered, but Laura was out of the den and in the foyer before Tincy could catch up with her.

She flung open the door, expecting the top-hatted, tails-wearing messenger with white gloves and a silver tray. But there was no sign of him or a Bugatti in the driveway. Instead, there was only a delivery van from Lexis Florist.

"Laura Bell?" a voice asked from behind a vase filled with snow white orchids and roses.

"Uh-huh."

"These are for you."

The flowers were carefully handed over, and Laura carried her haul into the kitchen, setting the vase down upon the granite-topped island. She peered into the cloudlike arrangement, looking for the card but turning up nothing.

"Who're they from?" Tincy asked, peering over her shoulder.

"I don't know." Laura shrugged.

"Guess you have a secret admirer," her mother teased.

"Maybe," Laura said, though she had the oddest sense she knew exactly who had sent them.

Avery.

Laura had no idea what was going on with him. After they'd spent the afternoon together on Saturday, she'd truly believed he was finally taking her feelings seriously. But catching him dropping off Camie Lindell at school yesterday morning had totally blindsided her. Even if driving Miss Camie had meant nothing to him, he hadn't tried very hard to set things straight. Unless these flowers were his way of asking for forgiveness. It was so Avery's style not to be direct.

Why'd I have to fall for a jock who plays games? she asked herself, not for the first time. But she had no answer. She never did. Sometimes love *happened* and there wasn't a damned thing you could do about it. Laura wasn't sure if she was stupid or crazy, but she wasn't giving up. Something in her heart wouldn't let her quit Avery yet. Or could be she was just an emotional masochist.

"They're so pretty!" Tincy exclaimed, taking Laura's hand and giving a squeeze right as the doorbell rang again.

Laura started at the noise and stared wide-eyed at Tincy.

"You want me to answer that?" her mother asked.

"Maybe it's just the florist with the missing card," Laura murmured, though even she didn't believe that. "I'll be right back."

Her mom nodded and let her go.

Laura walked slowly to the front hallway, rubbing her damp palms on the thighs of her jeans, the thud of her heartbeat loud in her chest. Drawing in a deep breath, she slowly opened the door to find herself standing face to face with Bootsie Bidwell in a St. John dress. On the driveway beyond was Bootsie's pristine white Cadillac.

She gulped.

Oh, hell, she thought, *this is it.* The committee chair had shown up to deliver a personal apology, to tell Laura how sorry she was that Laura hadn't made the cut. A pity visit: that was what it was, wasn't it?

Laura wanted to weep right then and there but managed to stay in control long enough to say in a well-mannered fashion, "Hello, Mrs. Bidwell."

Bootsie clutched her Prada bag with both hands, fiddling with the clasp. She cleared her throat before she said, "I wanted to drop by and give you this myself, after all you've been through these past twenty-four hours."

With that, she withdrew an envelope from her bag, crisp white linen with *Laura Delacroix Bell* across the front in the most elegant calligraphy.

"Open it, please," Bootsie urged, and Laura worked as fast as she could with trembling, nail-bitten fingers. "Good luck, hon," Jo Lynn's mother drawled, though her voice seemed suddenly far in the distance.

All Laura could see, all she could focus on, were the words engraved on the invitation:

You are cordially invited to
The Glass Slipper Club's
Welcome Dinner for our newest Rosebuds
Friday evening at seven o'clock
The Manor House
At the Houstonian

Kindly reply to Bootsie Bidwell,
Selection Committee Chair

"I'm in?" Laura asked, hardly believing it.

"Yes," Bootsie told her. "You're in. Congratulations."

Laura let out a shriek at the top of her lungs and threw her arms around a startled Mrs. Bidwell. All the while, she kept hearing a modified version of her mantra racing through her head: *I am who I am . . . and I'm in!*

And that was that.

Epilogue

Friday Evening
THE ROSEBUD DINNER

Laura had hardly been able to sleep or eat or *breathe* since Bootsie Bidwell had personally delivered her Rosebud invitation on Tuesday night. The rest of the week had raced by at lightning speed. Every spare minute was spent with Mac and Ginger, planning what to wear to the debutante dinner, how to do their hair, and how to smile like an ice princess when bumping into members of the Bimbo Cartel.

Though Laura had hardly forgotten about Avery, she wasn't going to let his obvious relapse back to the dark side ruin her night. Having attended an all-girls school since kindergarten had somehow made it easier to push aside thoughts of guys, and she did just that, clearing her head of negative things. Instead, she envisioned herself wearing the white deb gown she'd have Vera Wang create as she rode in her daddy's chauffeur-driven Bentley with her mother, heading to the Houstonian Hotel to celebrate double-D-Day (the Debutante Dinner).

Too nervous to do anything but chitchat idly with Tincy,

Laura fidgeted all the way to Post Oak, checking her lip gloss a million times, adjusting the straps on her shoes, playing with the hem of her dress.

In a blink, it seemed, they'd arrived, and her daddy's driver, Eldon, opened the door to the Bentley and extended a gloved hand.

"Mrs. Bell," Eldon said, his voice warbling, and Laura watched as Tincy slid out before her, exiting gracefully, so slim and tiny—and so sedate in pearl gray Armani.

Laura's father hadn't even been home to see her off, since he'd had to fly to Amsterdam on business, namely, taking over a Dutch company that would eventually make him even more millions in the plumbing business.

But Laura didn't care.

She was too elated to let anything bring her down. Besides, the only faces she wanted to see tonight belonged to Mac Mackenzie and Ginger Fore.

She wouldn't mind seeing the second Mrs. Mackenzie, either, and thanking her in person. If it weren't for Honey Potts, she'd be dead in the water. Whatever Mac's stepmummy had done—and Laura wasn't sure exactly what that was, as Honey hadn't told a soul—it had certainly worked.

Laura was just steps away from heading into the formal dinner, and she knew that, with her friends beside her, she could handle anything, even smiling graciously at Jo Lynn Bidwell and her toadies, Camie and Trisha, all the while wanting to wring their necks. But that day would come.

For now, she could hardly contain her happiness, which had seemed to grow exponentially the nearer they'd come to the Manor House on the hotel's lushly landscaped grounds.

She hadn't been able to hold back a tiny squeal when they'd pulled up to the doors.

As she waited for Eldon to finish helping her mother out, Laura smoothed down the skirt of her pink satin Shalini with a deep V-neck that showed off her boobage. She'd had it flown in from Bergdorf Goodman in New York after she'd seen it online. It hadn't even needed alterations, proof that it was fated to be hers. She glanced down at her polished pink toenails peeping out of the pair of Manolo Blahnik jeweled T-strap sandals that made her size elevens look so much smaller somehow.

The whole outfit was perfect, she knew, and she felt every bit like a modern-day Cinderella.

"Miss Bell?" Eldon was saying, probably not for the first time, and Laura's head snapped up.

"Oh, yeah. Sorry, El," she said and reached for his proffered hand, allowing him to help her from the car without stumbling and making a fool of herself or pulling a Britney (though Laura had her tummy-tucking Spanx on, so she wouldn't be flashing her private parts to anyone, not tonight, anyway).

A polished black Mercedes and a silver Jag pulled up behind the Bentley in front of the redbrick Manor House with its hunter green shutters that matched the green awning.

As she followed her mother to the entrance, she heard Eldon slap the car door closed behind her and the motor hum as he pulled away.

Laura took one last long, deep breath before leaving the quiet of outside for the noisy chatter of indoors.

"Tincy, darlin', and Laura dear, how lovely you both

look!" Bootsie Bidwell greeted them effusively, then passed them along to the line of selection committee members inside the door. They congratulated Laura, air-kissed her cheeks, and handed her a single white rose.

Laura lifted the flower to her nose, inhaling its sweetness, and she realized that the moment she'd waited for all her life was so near she could smell it as well.

The rooms swelled with voices, which rose above the background notes of the string quartet playing Mozart. Near the bar across from the fireplace, ladies milled about with drinks in hand, but Laura wandered toward the dining room with its multipaned windows giving views to the greenery outdoors.

The tables had been set with white linen and standing floral arrangements brimming with every kind of white flower imaginable.

She scanned the place settings until she found her name.

Laura Delacroix Bell, Rosebud, it read, and that alone sent a chill up her spine.

"I'm a deb," she said quietly, then said it again for good measure. "I'm an honest-to-God Glass Slipper Debutante."

"Oh, no, you aren't, Hostess Cupcake. Not yet. Not by a long shot."

Laura turned at the voice, finding Jo Lynn Bidwell standing not an arm's length away.

She held a white rose of her own, which blended in with her tight white dress embroidered in red. Laura hated that her nemesis looked so perfect in it, not a blond hair out of place, her makeup glamorous, and her smoky, smudged eyes as mean as a snake.

"What do you want?" Laura tried to stay cool despite

how much she hated merely looking at Jo Lynn's face. Though she ached to claw the bitch's eyes out with her manicured nail tips, she kept her hands to herself, desperate not to let anything spoil the night.

"I see you're wearing pink," Jo Lynn drawled. "That's a good color for a pig who likes to squeal. No one likes a tattletale."

"Or a blackmailer," Laura shot back, keeping her tone low and a smile on her lips so that no one around them could tell anything was wrong.

"You know Avery's back with Camie. She's forgiven him for straying."

Laura bit her tongue and refused to rise to the bait, no matter how much it hurt, how much she wanted to call Jo Lynn a liar.

"I'll bet it isn't easy for a girl like you to find a boyfriend who's faithful," Jo Lynn tried again, and this time Laura couldn't resist.

"Speaking of unfaithful boyfriends, did Dillon ever tell you where he went in such a hurry?" she replied, and Jo Lynn flinched. "Whatever his excuse was, I know I wouldn't believe it."

Jo Lynn crooked a finger, and Laura leaned in as close as she dared. "You listen to me, loser. I'll bring you down, one way or another. You don't deserve to be here, and I'll make sure you don't stay."

Laura wondered for an instant if it was against the rules of the debutante program to backhand a fellow Rosebud, but she figured it probably was.

She met Jo Lynn's eyes without blinking and told her through gritted teeth, "Bring it on."

"Um, hey, what's going on over here?"

It was Mac.

Jo Lynn drew back. "Nothing's going on. *Yet*," she hissed, giving Laura an icy glare before gliding off.

"Perfect timing," Laura breathed, her pulse easing back to normal. "Man, that witch has it coming."

Then she turned her attention fully on Mac, and her eyes widened. She couldn't help gawking. "My God, what happened to you?"

"Honey happened," her friend said, shifting on her strappy-sandaled feet. "I had to agree to let her prettify me to pay her back for what she did for you. So you owe me. Big-time."

Laura grinned, tapping Mac on the shoulder with her white rose. "Girl, I think I did you a favor. You look amazing."

And she did: all soft and girly instead of rough around the edges.

Mac's hair had been styled, her inky dark curls loosened by some very artful blow-drying, and her bangs had been layered so they were less severe and more feminine. Her thick brows had been plucked into more slender arches, opening up her eyes so they seemed even bigger than usual.

Laura squinted. "Are you wearing contact lenses?"

"It's a one-time thing, I swear." Mac made a face. "Having plastic on my eyeballs feels way too weird."

"You've got on lipstick, too."

"I know," Mac sighed. "I feel like a fraud."

Laura laughed. "Well, you don't look like one. You're a dead ringer for Zooey Deschanel."

Mac wrinkled her brow. "Is she new at PFP?"

"She's an actress, silly, and she's gorgeous."

"You're crazy."

"And you're blushing," Laura teased, because she was. She glanced over Mac's shoulder to catch another girl coming through the door, receiving a white rose from Bootsie Bidwell, and her jaw dropped. "Oh, my God."

"What?" Mac spun around to see what Laura was looking at. "Is that . . . ?"

"Ginger," they both said at once.

"She's done it again," Laura breathed. "The Green Girl has been possessed by a redheaded Sienna Miller."

Her bright orange hair had been tamed to a softer auburn color, and it no longer stuck up from her head in messy tufts. Her cut was modified pixie, and her makeup was all pinks and taupes. Her dress looked like a flashback, with its boho peasant appearance.

"Is this a new phase or just a momentary lapse?" Laura whispered to Mac as the third member of the newly formed and top-secret Bitch Haters Club approached. Mac elbowed her to make her shut up.

"Hi, y'all. So I guess we're all in, despite everything, huh? Are we totally insane, or what?" Ginger said by way of greeting, and Mac gave her a quick hug while Laura glanced across the room, spotting Camie and Trisha huddled with Jo Lynn.

"You mean, we're all in *if* we can make it through the next nine months," Laura said under her breath, holding tight to her white rose, wondering if the ten girls here tonight would be the same ten to do the Texas Dip in their gowns and gloves late next spring.

Like Jo Lynn had said: *It isn't over yet.*

Laura felt suddenly uneasy as she realized that making it through her deb season would be rougher than she'd thought, particularly with Jo Lynn and the Bimbo Cartel dreaming up ways to trip her up. She'd have to be on guard at all times, even strike first to stay one step ahead. And on top of all that, how the hell was she going to get Avery to come to his senses?

There was so much to consider.

But she couldn't let any of it ruin the dinner.

Screw the Bimbo Cartel, she thought, until the *ching-ching-ching* of sterling upon crystal caught her ear, and she looked to the front of the room to see Bootsie Bidwell gesturing.

"Good evening, everyone, may I have your attention," the chair of the Glass Slipper Club's selection committee drawled in a voice both loud and clear. "I very much want to introduce y'all to this season's ten Rosebuds, who'll debut in the spring, starting alphabetically with Miss Laura Delacroix Bell. Would you come to the front of the room, Laura, please?"

It's really happening, Laura thought, hearing the polite applause as she took one step forward and then another, her heart beating faster, knowing there was no turning back.

Whatever happened after tonight . . . well, hell, she'd think about that tomorrow.

ACKNOWLEDGMENTS

I wasn't sure how easy it would be to go from writing a mystery series to spinning stories about debutantes in my hometown of Houston, Texas. Dealing with raw emotions and real-life relationships is worlds apart from devising clever ways to kill (on paper, I mean). But I've enjoyed every minute I've spent with Laura, Mac, Ginger, and Jo Lynn (aka "The Debs"), and I feel very fortunate that this opportunity came up when it did. For that, I have my agent, the fabulous Kelly Harms, to thank, as well as Claudia Gabel, my amazing editor at Delacorte Press. Now I'll just cross my fingers and hope that readers love these stories and these girls as much as I do.

Coming in June 2009

The Debs:
Love, Lies, and Texas Dips

Where is everyone?

Jo Lynn Bidwell entered the Houstonian's Grande Ballroom in a rustle of tulle petticoats and silk. She'd expected to hear music, to see the arch of raised military sabers that she was supposed to walk beneath on her daddy's arm when she was formally introduced, but the enormous room was dead silent.

"Hello?"

Despite the elbow-length white kidskin gloves, goose bumps rose on her arms, and she rubbed them as she wandered around, gazing up at the chandeliers that dripped from the ceiling. The crystal-beaded lamps were bare, without the clouds of white dendrobium orchids Bootsie Bidwell had said would be flown in from Hawaii to decorate the room for the Rosebud Ball. Jo noticed too that the tables had no linens, and there were folding chairs parked around them. *Where are the gold Chiavari chairs and the enormous floral centerpieces that Bootsie had specially designed by Lyman Ratcliffe?* They were nowhere in sight.

"Hello?" she repeated, though her voice merely echoed in the huge space. "Is anyone here?"

She glanced around, catching her reflection in a mirror on the wall—then realizing it wasn't her reflection at all. The girl in the silvered glass was at least twice her size, and she was smiling maliciously as she approached.

Oh, hell, it was Laura Bell, wearing the exact same white Vera Wang gown Jo Lynn had donned: a silk satin underlay with a layer of English netting and a silk voile overlay with delicate hand-sewn flower appliqués and seed pearls. Except Laura's dress was obviously much larger than Jo Lynn's. Forget her being a debu-tank. She was more like a debu-blimp, as in Goodyear.

"Surprise, surprise," Laura taunted her, the sparkle from the heavily jeweled tiara in her upswept blond hair so intense Jo felt blinded. "What's wrong, girlfriend?" Laura's square-jawed face leaned close enough for Jo to feel the girl's hot breath on her skin. "You look like you've seen a ghost. Or is it just envy, since I look better in this gown than you? Or is it because I've got the best-looking escort in the room and you're all by your lonesome?"

Jo Lynn started to open her mouth to fight back, but all words caught in her throat when she saw the broad-shouldered guy in the tuxedo walking toward them. He ignored Jo completely as he took Laura's hand.

OMG. It was Dillon Masters.

Her Dillon.

"Noooooooo!" Jo Lynn screamed at the top of her lungs.

Hands gripped her, shaking her shoulders, and a gravelly voice said, "Jo, hey, calm down. It's all right."

But it isn't all right. Dillon is with that lard-ass Laura!

Jo struggled against the arms that wrapped tightly around her. A sob wedged in her throat, and she felt the rush of tears dammed behind her eyelids.

"Baby, I'm here. It's okay."

She stopped fighting and finally forced her eyes open to see Dillon's face. His wide brow was wrinkled with concern. She wiped the dampness from her cheeks and touched his jaw, the unshaved skin like sandpaper, then let out a huge sigh of relief.

"You're here," she whispered, and glanced around at the familiar living room of her family's guesthouse. They lay on the L-shaped sofa, across from the plasma TV, its screen dark and empty. It had all been a dream, she realized, the crazy beat of her heart slowing down. *This* was real. How could she ever have believed someone like Dillon would be with a slob like Laura?

"Oh, God," she cried, and threw herself into his arms. "It was awful."

"I knew we shouldn't have watched *Sean of the Dead* again," he said as he stroked her hair. "All that salsa and chips probably didn't help either, and neither did falling asleep on the couch." He squinted at his wristwatch and groaned. "It's nearly eight."

"But it's Labor Day, Dil. No school, remember?"

"Your mom's gonna freak if she wakes up and sees my car at this hour."

"Please," Jo scoffed. "Bootsie adores you."

And it was true. Her mother *loved* Dillon. She'd totally buy that they'd passed out in the guesthouse watching movies, which was really all they'd done. Bootsie thought Jo Lynn's boyfriend, Mr. Star Quarterback, was the model gentleman, and he was, even closer to perfect than Jo Lynn would've liked—although he *had* macked on her plenty last night. It was almost like he was out to prove himself after the romantic drought they endured the past few months, which Dillon blamed on the stress of football practice, training sessions, and pressure from his dad and college recruiters.

"You had a nightmare, huh?" he asked, settling back against the deep cushions, his pale eyes watching her.

He obviously isn't in a hurry to disappear, Jo thought smugly, hoping that things were getting back to normal. She'd missed being close to him. She wanted the weirdness between them gone.

"More like a fright-mare," she said, shaking off the flashes of it that still lingered. She squeezed her eyes closed a couple of times to clear her visions. "I was at the Houstonian, but no one else was there for the deb ball except that skank Laura Bell, and she was wearing *my* couture Vera Wang gown, although hers was *way* bigger than mine, of course, but that couldn't possibly happen because the Glass Slipper Club's historian records everyone's dresses so no two are alike—"

Dillon was staring at her like she was a lunatic, so she stopped herself. "Never mind," she told him, because explaining it did make her sound totally obsessive. "I think I'm just feeling some pressure. The first Rosebud meeting's tomorrow night, and *she'll* be there, acting like she's all that and getting in my face unless I—"

Jo Lynn didn't finish. Dillon didn't need to hear about her scheme to get Laura ousted from the Rosebuds no matter what it took. She gnawed on her lower lip for a few moments, wanting to ask him a question that nagged at her.

Finally, as nonchalantly as she could, she said "Just out of curiosity, what do you think of her?"

"Who?"

"Laura Bell," she said slowly, practically spelling the name out.

Dillon shrugged. "I don't know her that well, except from when Avery used to bring her around, but she seems okay."

That wasn't exactly what Jo Lynn was getting at, so she went right for the jugular: "You don't think she's attractive, do you?"

Her boyfriend drew back, giving her a "what the hell?" look. "Why would you even ask that?"

Because you were her escort for the deb ball in my damned dream, Jo nearly blurted out, but checked herself. "Like you said, Avery went out with her, and I thought he had better taste than that. She's . . . supersized."

"Do you hate her because he was your boyfriend first? That's what bugs you the most, isn't it? He went from dating you to seeing a girl who's definitely not your idea of a beauty queen." Dillon sighed, and the muscles in his jaw twitched. "Jesus, Jo. I'm surprised you let someone like Laura Bell get under your skin so much that you're having nightmares about her."

"You don't understand," Jo Lynn snapped.

"No, I don't understand at all. You have everything any girl could want, but instead of being happy you keep fixating on someone who can't hold a candle to you." Dillon sighed again, staring at her, and there was something in his eyes that caused a chill to settle between them. "You need to give it a rest."

That got Jo's back up. "So I'm a bitch for not liking her, is that it?"

Dillon looked at her for a long time before he said quietly, "Sometimes I'm just not sure what I've gotten myself into."

What was that supposed to mean?

Is it because I brought up Avery? Is he jealous? she wondered.

Or was it something else?

Don't push it, Jo, she told herself, and her mind quickly shifted into gear. She hurried to fix things, before all the warm, fuzzy feelings from their evening together evaporated.

"Look, I'm sorry. I don't want to fight. Seriously, I should thank you for hanging with me. *All* night," she added, leaving out the rest of what she was thinking, namely, *Even if we didn't actually* do *it.*

Jo Lynn leaned over and pressed her lips to Dillon's, tasting his morning breath and not caring a bit. He pulled away and held her shoulders.

"No, I should be thanking you," Dillon said, "for getting that I need to slow things down a little. Sometimes it feels like everything's moving so fast around me that I can't think straight." He shook his head, exhaling slowly, and Jo Lynn reached up to curl her fingers around his arms.

"Uh, yeah, sure it's okay," she reassured him, though she didn't exactly mean it. She wasn't at all certain about this "I want to take things slow" gobbledygook. *When did I agree to that?* It was more like *he'd* slowed down all on his own this past summer, after a year of going hot and heavy, and the only thing she could do to hold on to him now was to go along with whatever he wanted.

So far as she knew, he hadn't been born again, and it was for damned sure she wasn't into reconstituted virginity. She'd heard of girls accepting some kind of creepy promise ring from their dads for pledging to swear off sex until marriage. Ugh. Besides, it was *way* too late for that. Avery had made sure of it. Weren't guys the ones who always wanted to move faster? As much as she wanted to ignore it, Dillon's need to put on the brakes didn't make sense.

"I really should go," Dillon said abruptly, and wriggled out of her grasp. He jumped up from the sofa. "I need to work out this morning before I help my folks get ready for later." He ran a hand over his tousled blond curls and looked around as he hiked up his cargo shorts and buttoned his vintage bowling shirt. "You know where my shoes are?" he asked, getting down on his hands and knees as he poked beneath the couch for his missing Vans.

Jo Lynn got a nice bird's-eye view of his butt as he bent over, and she smiled as she watched him scrounge around for his kicks. It was almost too bad when he found them.

"I'll see you at one o'clock, yeah?" Dillon slipped on his shoes. "You're coming to my folks' annual barbecue, right? My dad would kill me if you didn't show. I think he's got a crush on you," he added, and wiggled his eyebrows.

"Stop it." Jo shook her head, grinning. He could be such a goof. "Of course I'll be there. I'm looking forward to it," she said, and meant it.

"Cool." He nodded as he stuck his wallet into his back pocket and picked up his cell from the coffee table without bothering to check it for messages. Then he grabbed his keys and headed for the door.

Jo Lynn shoved her feet into her favorite floral-embroidered

Christian Lacroix flats and snatched up her iPhone, which she'd turned off last night so nothing would interrupt them. Hopping off the sofa, she followed him to the door. She flipped her tangled blond hair behind her shoulders, coming up behind him as he paused before leaving.

"Bye, babe, I'll see you this afternoon," he said, kissing her gently before he loped down the steps toward his red Mustang.

Jo closed the door and stood on the porch, listening to the sports car roar to life, the engine growling as it pulled away. She suddenly realized Dillon had never actually answered her question about whether he found Laura Bell attractive.

I'm surprised you let someone like Laura get under your skin, she heard him saying, and she hated the fact that he was right. She shook off her attack of insecurity, something she'd rarely felt since she'd had to give up pageants after her sophomore year.

Of course Dillon didn't think Laura was pretty, she told herself. The girl was as tall as an Amazon and had a body type Bootsie politely referred to as "sturdy." Not to mention she had no manners at all. Laura was known throughout Pine Forest Prep for saying precisely what she thought without thinking first and often ended up with her hefty size-eleven foot in her mouth. They might both be trust-fund babies, but that was *all* they had in common. Well, except the fact that they were both blondes and their mothers were best friends . . . and, unfortunately, Laura had also been picked by the Glass Slipper Club to be one of ten Pine Forest Prep senior girls in this season's debutante class.

Though if Jo Lynn could find a way to get Miss Ding-

Dong Bell booted out of the Rosebuds on her "sturdy" ass, she was bound and determined to do it. She'd already played an ace—or what she'd assumed was an ace—when she'd anonymously messengered a photo of a drunk and disrobed Laura Bell to every woman on the GSC's debutante selection committee. Surprisingly that had backfired, leaving Jo Lynn with no choice but to try something else—which reminded her that she had some work to do on her "Get Laura Booted from the Buds" project before Dillon's family barbecue this afternoon. It *was* Labor Day, after all, wasn't it? Only, this chore would be fun.

Jo Lynn turned on her iPhone and found she had a new text message. She paused on the flagstone path that led around the pool to the main house, went to her SMS screen and read Camie Lindell's note. Her friend was obviously curious about how things had gone with Jo and Dillon.

So??? Whassup with U and Big D?

Jo smiled and texted back: He just left.

Camie's reply bounced back like she'd been sitting on her cell, waiting for Jo to respond. No way!!!

Way! Jo tapped into the keypad. And I'll C him L8R at his BBQ. I so heart him!

You suck! I'll B hanging out with Trish while U have real fun. We're going 2 the country club 4 yoga, lunch & mani-pedis. Spill ALL when U get back!!!

U know I will.

My BFFs will have to do without me today, Jo mused as she slipped her phone into her back pocket and strode across the flagstone walkway through the manicured lawn. Though she was usually too preoccupied to admire the pretty acre in Houston's pricey Piney Point Village upon which sat the home her daddy had custom-built before she was born, she took it in now. Tall pines soared heavenward and enclosed the property, hugging its borders like giant guardians, keeping the Bidwells safely separated from the rest of the world. Graceful cypresses dripped Spanish moss; fluffy asparagus ferns flourished; and the hibiscus, oleander, and Mexican honeysuckle still bloomed wildly in early September. Sago palms looked like verdant umbrellas, while velvet-leaved princess flower bushes still bore a few deep purple blooms.

Jo inhaled deeply, the sweet mix of scents so pervasive on the humid air that she could almost taste them.

Today, she decided then and there, *will be absolutely perfect. Nothing and no one can ruin it.*

Having the day off from school after two weeks back at good ol' all-girls PFP rocked, particularly since it meant she'd be spending the afternoon with Dillon. Even though she wished they were doing something alone and not having to play nice with Dillon's parents, plus most of the Caldwell Academy football team. Still, Jo Lynn kind of liked it when she got to act like Dillon's arm candy, and he seemed to enjoy showing her off to the other guys, like he'd won a big prize that they'd never get.

Texas men were kind of possessive that way, even the well-bred ones who'd been reared in River Oaks or the Memorial Villages with silver spoons in their mouths and Gucci saddles beneath their butts. For sure, Dillon Masters was no redneck. He didn't like to hunt, for one, and he didn't do chaw, wear Lucchese boots day in and day out, or drive a pickup (with or without a gun rack) with that omnipresent bumper sticker that read DON'T MESS WITH TEXAS.

Not that Jo Lynn didn't appreciate the motto, because she did. She kind of wished the whole world heeded the warning of "Don't mess with Jo Lynn Bidwell," though it was pretty much unwritten law at PFP that most girls seemed inclined to obey. At least, the ones who knew what was good for them.

There was one woman, though, who intimidated Jo Lynn, and it wasn't a prep school rival or any competitor she'd ever encountered on the pageant scene, but rather Bootsie Bidwell, her mother, who just happened to be this year's chair of the GSC debutante selection committee. And Jo Lynn didn't want to cause an early-morning stink with her mother for strolling in at breakfast time, even if she'd spent the night only yards away in the family's guesthouse with the Golden Boy of Caldwell Academy, whom she had every intention of marrying one day.

Jo used her key to open the door to the main house and stepped into a rear hallway near the utility room, just past the butler's pantry, where kitchen deliveries were received.

She heard the familiar noises of pots and pans clanking in the granite and stainless steel kitchen as Bootsie's personal chef prepared weekend brunch, always served promptly at eleven. Jo figured Cookie was getting double pay for sticking around and feeding the Bidwells on a holiday when even the housekeeper, Nan, had been cut loose for Labor Day. Not that Jo minded, since it meant the house would smell like cinnamon and other spices all morning.

Not wanting to attract Cookie's attention, Jo removed her shoes, dangling them from her fingers as she tiptoed past the kitchen and scurried across the foyer, the marble floor cold beneath her feet. She briefly glanced up at the impossibly high painted ceiling—Bootsie's ode to Michelangelo's frescoes in the Sistine Chapel—and took the curving stairwell up to her bedroom as quietly as possible, avoiding the floorboards that creaked beneath the Oriental runner just outside her parents' bedroom. She had one hand on the knob of the door to her bedroom suite and was about to turn it when a voice from behind startled her.

"I think you missed your curfew," Bootsie said, her honey-eyed drawl laced with sarcasm.

Please. As if I actually have a curfew.

Jo Lynn slowly turned to face her. "Good morning, Mother."

Her mom gave her a slow once-over, and Jo knew she looked a mess. Her makeup was doubtless smeared, and she was wearing the same pair of hip-hugging D&G jeans and pleated white shirt she'd had on last night when she'd gone out to eat with Dillon, only now she looked severely wrinkled. Her fabric flats were damp with dew. As usual, Bootsie appeared the model nouveau-riche mummy, a tribute to crisp perfection even at barely half past eight in her tailored pearl gray Chanel slacks and sage green silk side-wrap blouse. She'd always been the best-dressed mother on the pageant scene, and Jo rarely saw her with a hair out of place.

Jo shifted on her feet, uncomfortable beneath Bootsie's critical gaze.

"Good thing I'm not doing pageants anymore, huh? I wouldn't even win Miss Junior Oil Refinery looking like this," Jo Lynn remarked, hating the length of her mother's silence. It meant Bootsie's brain was making a list of Jo Lynn's imperfections, like she'd done back in Jo's pageant days.

"You do look a mess," Bootsie said, crossing her arms and tilting her head. "But I guess that's what happens when you don't sleep in your own bed."

Jo Lynn squirmed but couldn't escape.

"Did Dillon stay over?" her mother asked, point-blank. "And don't lie, because I heard a noise a few minutes ago and I caught his car pulling out of the drive."

"It was no big deal, really," Jo mumbled. "We fell asleep in the guesthouse watching movies." Well, it was the truth. She just left out the part about them messing around, because no mother alive wanted to think her daughter put out for anyone, even Mr. Perfect, Dillon Masters. "I've got some stuff to do before his parents' party this afternoon," she said, meeting her mother's eyes as she inched her bedroom door open. "So if you'll excuse me . . ."

"You be careful, baby girl," Bootsie said, and caught her by the shoulder, holding on firmly. "The Glass Slipper Club takes their debutantes very seriously, and you know the rules. Any public indiscretion could cost you your position."

Public indiscretion?

"It's not like we were getting it on in the street, Mother, for God's sake," Jo Lynn grumbled. "If anyone spreads any nasty gossip about me or Dillon, it'll just be because they're jealous."

But the warning look didn't leave Bootsie's narrowed eyes. "I'm serious, baby. You need to watch yourself. All it takes is one unforgivable slip, and the GSC will review your Rosebud status. If that happens, I won't be able to do a thing about it. We've already had to terminate one girl, and it hasn't been pleasant."

"Who?" Jo Lynn perked up, hoping against all hope it was that fat blob Laura Bell.

Bootsie gave a little shake of her head. "Now, Jo, you know I can't discuss that with you. You'll find out soon enough, I'm sure. Besides, it's not anyone else's daughter I'm worried about. It's you."

"You don't have to worry about me, I swear. It won't be me who slips, I promise you," Jo Lynn insisted, but Bootsie didn't look completely reassured.

Bootsie nodded, giving her shoulder a squeeze before she released her. "Why don't you get cleaned up, and I'll see you at brunch at eleven? Jacques has a new stuffed French toast he's trying out on us this morning, and a soufflé with green peppers and caviar."

"Egg soufflé with caviar?" Jo Lynn made a face, and Bootsie laughed.

"You can stick to the French toast."

"I do believe I will," Jo said, watching her mother stride down the Oriental runner toward the stairs. Then she pushed into her room and shut the door, locking it behind her. She had something to take care of before she showered and made herself presentable for brunch.

She dumped her shoes on the floor and slid into her cane-backed desk chair. Settling in front of her wide-screen flat-panel monitor, she palmed her mouse, which was yellow and shaped like a VW Bug. When she clicked on it, tiny headlights lit up and it beeped. She pulled up a book-marked page and prepared to place an order, her third in the past few weeks. Last time, it was for Godiva. This time, it was for two dozen brownies from the Fairytale Bakery. Just for the hell of it, she added a Caramel Endings dessert sauce and a bag of cashews. *How many calories are in those suckers?* she wondered. *Like, a million?*

Enough, she was sure, to lead the already oversized Laura Bell on a course to debutante destruction, if she wasn't already on the fast track to an early exit. *We'll see if big girls do cry,* Jo Lynn thought, pulling out her prepaid debit card, the one she'd bought with cash so there'd be no way to link it back to her. She smiled as she clicked on "Order Now."

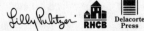